# Love Under Lockdown

by

## Michael Estorick

A

ARCADIA

Arcadia Books Ltd
139 Highlever Road, London W10 6PH
www.arcadiabooks.co.uk

First published in the United Kingdom by Arcadia Books 2021

A catalogue record for this book is available from the British Library.

ISBN: 978-1-911350-98-9

Designed and produced by Simon Rendall
typeset in Cardea and printed by TJ Books, of Padstow

Arcadia Books distributors are as follows:

*in the UK and elsewhere in Europe:*
Scottish Booksource
50 Cambuslang Road, Glasgow G32 8NB

*in the USA and Canada:*
Bookmasters
30 Amberwood Parkway, Ashland OH 44805

*in Australia/New Zealand:*
NewSouth Books
University of New South Wales, Sydney NSW 2052

*for Maurice Gee*

'What do you think?' Bill asked, for once wanting his oldest friend's opinion.

'Very artistic,' Pete said.

'No, seriously.'

'I am serious. I'm impressed. But what exactly are they?'

The two men were standing over a group of large black and white photographs of circular abstract patterns, taken by Bill.

Early on Midsummer morning, unable to sleep, Bill had gone down to the cellar to pick out a bottle with which to celebrate or drown his sorrows, depending on the outcome of the Brexit Referendum. On the landing outside there had been a smell of damp and at the bottom of the steps wine labels were strewn across the floor. Overnight, water had surged up through the sewers and then drained away, leaving large grey marks on the concrete.

'I think they're beautiful.'

'They are,' Pete said, and meant it.

'Of course, there's no way they're accidental.'

Oh God, Pete thought, not Bill and his crop circles again.

'They're too perfectly symmetrical.'

'Bill, they're just shapes made by water swirling around. That's all they are. Really.'

'It's no accident it happened right before the Referendum, like that terrible storm on the eve of Oliver Cromwell's death in 1658. An augury, if you like.'

Pete looked sharply at Bill, who knew Cromwell was his pet subject; or rather Richard, his son and successor as Lord Protector, commonly known as 'Tumbledown Dick', the only British ruler ever to give up power voluntarily and live to a contented old age.

'Not just a leak from the mains then?'

'Definitely not!'

'A leak from the Main Man, showing what he thinks of us – well, you anyway – by pissing on us from a great height?'

'Something like that, yes.'

'Yeah, right,' Pete said, shaking his head.

Bill was given to all-consuming passions, and before his 'awakening' five years earlier ('Trust Bill to big-up a plain old mid-life crisis,' his late wife Carol had said) would strenuously argue that crop circles were a con, two fingers stuck up at credulous New Agers by mocking farmers or smart-arse students. Extensive on-line research had subsequently persuaded Bill that they could only have been made by exceptionally intelligent extra-terrestrial visitors; and when, later still, his original view was vindicated, he perversely insisted that they must be the product of some supreme overarching intelligence by which the universe in all its particulars, both infinitely large and infinitesimally small, was ordered. Carol had never tolerated unscientific claptrap, any more than it would have occurred to her to vote, as Bill had just done, to leave Europe. Though he missed his wife every day and had barely moved a thing of hers since her death three years earlier, he was relieved she wasn't around, for he knew it was an argument he could never have won; nor, in all likelihood, despite all they had been through together, would their marriage, like so many others up and down the country in the wake of that historic vote, have survived it.

'Well, they make jolly nice snaps.'

'Snaps?' Bill said, feigning annoyance. 'Them's bleedin' art mate. The real effing deal. None of your conceptual bollocks.'

'Indeed,' Pete said.

'As a tribute to you I'm calling them Closely Observed Stains.'

Closely Observed Trains was Pete's favourite film. Pete bowed.

'I didn't know you were into photography.'

'There's a lot you don't know about me.'

'Not that much,' Pete thought, but said nothing

Pete liked to think he knew Bill better than Bill knew himself. They'd met 55 years before, aged 10, at a school entrance exam and been friends ever since. Though at times both had wondered what they saw in each other, neither had ever felt any need to explain or define a relationship which was a bouillabaisse of habit, shared experience, prejudice, insight, self-delusion, envy, competitiveness and general wear and tear. There had been long periods when they'd seen little of each other, and others when they'd been inseparable. Bill was given to teasing Pete, and probably enjoyed Pete's company more than the reverse, but it was invariably Pete who made any arrangement to meet. Both were now retired, Bill after successfully selling his advertising agency; Pete, if an artist can ever be said to retire, unexpectedly forced out of teaching by a new art school principal keen to give jobs to his mates. Bill had been married to Carol for over 30 years and had two daughters and a son. Five years earlier, aged 60, Pete had married for the first time (to Sarah, to whom he'd been introduced by Carol, thus becoming a step-father to seven-year-old Jack), but for reasons Pete claimed not to understand, they were no longer together. Bill was given to temporary enthusiasms and fads; Pete, a printmaker by training and vocation, steadier in his pursuits, though in their private lives the opposite was true: Bill, until his mid-life crisis, a devoted husband and father; Pete, before his late marriage, a loner as promiscuous in his affections as he was protective of his heart. After Carol's death from cancer and Pete's separation from Sarah, the two men had briefly shared Bill's spacious house in Wimbledon. Bill had then fallen for Andrea, a rapacious American divorcee, to whom he'd been introduced by Pete, but to general relief – Pete's especially – she had stood him up at the altar. At the time of the Brexit Referendum in June 2016, both Pete and Bill were single and living alone, though they met for lunch every Tuesday at the Fox & Grapes by Wimbledon Common.

From time to time Bill's son Ivan, now in his mid-20's, would turn up unannounced, suitcase and heart in hand, and re-install himself in the bedroom in which he'd grown up. Or not, as Bill insisted to Pete, who was his godfather. A couple of days after the vote, Ivan appeared, accompanied by a young woman called Melanie, with gold rings through her nose and eyebrow, and an indecipherable tattoo above her breasts which Bill couldn't take his eyes off.

'Don't say anything, Dad. It's nothing like that,' Ivan insisted, when she went to the lavatory.

'Like what?'

'Mel and me, we're like just friends, OK?'

'Sorry to hear that.'

'And stop salivating. It's disgusting at your age.'

'I was trying to read her tattoo.'

'Sure you were.'

'How long's she staying?'

Ivan shrugged.

'For a bit. She needs somewhere to hang.'

'Hang what?'

Before Ivan could explain, Melanie came back into the room.

'They're fascists,' she announced, to no one in particular.

'Who?'

'My progenitors.'

'Your what?'

'Her parents, Dad.'

'Oh, right. Sorry.'

'Mel couldn't stay at home after the way they voted. Well, how could anyone?'

'I've no idea,' Bill said.

'So it might be a few days or a few weeks. All right?' Ivan added, more a statement than question.

'Sure. Make yourselves at home.'

'Great. Thanks.'

Mel didn't open her mouth again, but as they went upstairs Bill noticed they were holding hands, and grinned lasciviously.

'I'm hardly surprised,' Bill told Pete. 'I'm not saying I expected it, but Brits don't like being told what to do, especially by bloody Yanks. It gets our blood up. The funny thing is, although I wanted us to leave, on hearing the result I felt rather flat. But winning's like that. You think it's going to feel like nothing on earth, when all it is is better than losing.'

'It must be nice having Ivan back,' Pete said. He was very fond of his godson and, unlike most people, had no interest in talking about the Brexit Referendum. Bill had always found his son a mystery and would often ask Pete for advice, even when he had no intention of taking it.

'He must know how I voted.'

'Maybe he doesn't care. Or likes his creature comforts too much to rock the boat. How about Mel?'

'Little Miss Tattoo behaves as if I don't exist. The fridge is now stuffed with the most awful vegan muck, and when-ever she sees me eating a ham sandwich she makes these appalling gagging noises. That's about the extent of her conversation.'

'They mean well,' Pete said, for he had always had a soft spot for students.

'Bollocks. They just want us to pack up and die.'

'Not really.'

'Yes, really. The other day I caught Ivan wandering round the house photographing everything on his phone.'

'Did you give him any tips?'

'It isn't funny.'

'Oh, I don't know. What did you say?'

'Nothing. I was too gobsmacked. But he knew what I was thinking. As for little Miss T, I don't think it's quite as platonic as he makes out, if the noises coming from his room are anything to go by. The funny thing is, she'd be a pretty little number if she didn't always look as if she'd just stepped out of the Amazon rainforest.'

'Bill, you can't say stuff like that these days. It's totally unacceptable.'

'Who says? This is still my house, isn't it? An Englishman's home...'

'Not for long, evidently!' Pete said, grinning.


## 2


Pilgrims had been on the road since dawn. Coffee in hand, Guy would watch them from the battlements, their backs bent under heavy packs, the occasional lone figure breaking ranks as he strode on ahead, crook in hand, towards the nearest town and breakfast.

In earlier years, pilgrims had straggled on an overgrown path across the field towards Guy's tower, but historic rights of way had been sold off and nowadays they kept to the road: a reciprocal deal between landowner and local government, from which Guy had gained or lost a few metres, he could no longer remember which, and cared even less.

In need of fresh water or a lavatory, one of them would occasionally call up or bang on the heavy front door. Guy, reluctant to be bothered, would peer down through one of the arrow slits. If the pilgrim was pretty he might open up; otherwise he refused to answer. On market days, he drove his old Peugeot dangerously close to the pilgrims, furious when they didn't move over; on his return journey, fresh baguette, farm eggs, goats cheese, a spit roasted chicken or *rôti de porc*, bouncing on the back seat, hypocritically raising a hand from the steering wheel in greeting. Guy despised organised religion and everything he imagined the pilgrims believed, but he envied them their freedom, even if it was only from an office for a couple of weeks a year. Now in his mid 60's, he more than ever missed the open road, wandering in remote places without guide or destination, having never imagined that a tumbledown tower, spotted through an overgrown hedge more than 40 years earlier, would one day become the only home he ever owned.

By midday it was too hot to walk. Pilgrims would be stretched out under the trees, eating or dozing or playing with their mobile phones. Guy took his second cup of coffee and tin of roll ups, and climbed the forty-two slippery stone steps, pitted and polished by centuries of wear, up onto the roof; from where, like some medieval seigneur, he would gaze proprietorially over vineyards and sunflowers and gently rolling hills, south towards the Pyrenees, pasted flat against the horizon like strips of torn paper.

His work finished until evening, Guy could now devote himself to his son Luke, six years old and younger than his granddaughter by a former wife. They might swim in the river or knock golf balls into the orchard, Guy torn between instructing and admiring the freedom with which Luke moved. Sports had once come easily to Guy. At school, many had envied the shots he'd played and passes made, but games had never mattered much to him; no more than had winning prizes or being part of a group. For though not an only child, he had always felt like one.

Every generation discovers the world for itself; remakes, as it were, a world created entirely by others, until it becomes its own. Guy had never understood his father's possessiveness or need to belong; never appreciated the aspirations of the immigrant or refugee. All he could see was his own need to break away and become himself. Unlike his father, Guy had also never viewed children as an extension of himself; and only on becoming a father for the second time in middle age, had he begun to appreciate what his own father, escaping to England from Nazi Germany in the late 1930s, must have felt. But by then it was too late. From the day Guy walked out of Cambridge at the end of his first year, his father had refused ever to speak to him again.

At the time, Guy's family had no idea that he meant to quit university; nor, until the end of that Long Vacation, had Guy. At the start of the holiday he had driven to Paris in his Triumph Herald with two fellow students – Bill from his college, and Bill's schoolfriend Pete, who was at art school in London – where, after a couple of days heavy drinking, he had abandoned them. He hadn't asked himself why he was leaving, any more than he knew where he was going, only that he had to get away. Perhaps it was Bill's evident, if unstated, demands on him, the way Bill presumed Guy had a better grasp of the world than he did; that look of hope, quickly followed by disappointment, whenever Guy failed to meet Bill's excessive expectations. Guy's father's demands were onerous enough, and the last thing Guy wanted – indeed, had ever wanted – was to be put on a pedestal. So at dawn, without a word, he had taken off and driven south, with no idea where he was going or hoped to end up. Just outside Paris, he picked up a pair of German hitchhikers, full of hippie gibberish, but had soon got rid of them. Whatever he was looking for, whatever he was hoping to find, could only be done on his own.

A couple of days later, among the cosy valleys of Armagnac, then a scarcely populated region of small, enclosed fields and derelict hamlets, he happened upon a medieval tower, abandoned and roofless, strangled by ivy, overlooking a stream and the remains of a mill. Without knowing why, Guy drove straight to the nearest town and searched out the estate agent, to find out if it was for sale; and, if not, to let him know if it ever was. To act without self-consciousness or preconception had always been Guy's aim; apart from his tower, property and possessions had never meant anything to him; people, outside his immediate circle, little more.

Being cut off by his father did nothing to bring Guy to heel; rather the reverse. Feeling he no longer had to perform had been wonderfully liberating. Guy never understood why people thought him stuck up or superior because he refused to meet their expectations. His expectations of himself were more than enough for one person and one lifetime.

Guy regretted not having talked more to Pete about art, but Bill's intrusive presence had made that impossible. There were questions he needed to ask; that would, in the event, take a lifetime to answer. Guy had a sharp, analytical brain and made connections readily, but that meant nothing in itself, for as yet he had no idea what he was looking for, or how to go about finding it. He was adept at capturing a physical likeness on paper, but, as in other things which came easily to him, was suspicious of his own facility. Drawing by-passed the intellect, which in itself appealed to Guy. But when, still a virgin, he'd joined a Cambridge life-drawing class, he'd been so distracted by the model that he'd felt compelled to leave, and never gone back.

After visiting the estate agent, he'd returned to the tower for one last look. He took no photographs, made no sketches, perhaps because it had made such a powerful impression. Then he drove westwards to Bordeaux. It was August 1971, and the city was deserted. He finally found a cheap hotel and a bistro by the port ringed by tarts, where for ten francs he could eat four courses with wine. Never happier than on his own, he had spent a week exploring the quiet, unrestored town, discovering the hazy, evocative city-scapes of a local artist, Albert Marquet, and an ideal of painting as something quiet and understated, without cleverness or trickery, susceptibilities he was only too aware of in himself.

By the time he got back to London he'd made up his mind. Returning to Cambridge for another two years would be, he was convinced, the biggest imposture of all.


3


'Guy won't welcome the result,' Pete said to Bill, over a pint at the pub. Bill shrugged.

'He probably doesn't even know it's happened. He's always had his head in the clouds.'

'The art school in its infinite wisdom got rid of him at the same time as me. Bloody fools. But he didn't seem to mind. He was never comfortable teaching and only did it as a favour to me. I assume he's back in France. He's got a great set-up there.'

'Stuck up his ivory tower, no doubt. I don't know why you went on teaching for so long,' Bill added, wanting to change the subject. Even now, he never felt comfortable talking about Guy.

'I enjoyed it. I like the young.'

'That's because you never had kids of your own. Try listening to them.'

'I do. We weren't any different in our day.'

'I was.'

'Yes, well. You've always been a one-off.'

Bill smiled, then shook his head again.

'I can't understand an effing word they say. That's if they ever deign to talk to me.'

'They probably think you're not listening.'

'I'm not.'

Pete went over to the bar to refill their glasses. In a loud voice, Bill said: 'Little Miss Muffet's got Ivan by the gonads. The other night I found him gazing forlornly into the fridge. We now have labels on everything in different coloured inks. Not that I'd want to eat any of that muck. And three rubbish bins instead of one, all because she insists we separate everything before putting it out. Rubbish, for Christ's sake.'

Pete was secretly pleased. Bill was always at his best when he had something to rail against, the less important the better. He was a generous, kind-hearted man, and with Carol his bluster had been mainly an act. He had always known when to back down, when a position was indefensible, when to retreat and regroup. It had been a close-run thing, but when, aged 60, he'd suddenly shed five stone and gone off spouting new-age nonsense, she'd called his bluff and after only a few weeks he'd returned home. Even in his new streamlined incarnation Bill liked his creature comforts too much to stay away for long.

'Ivan seems happy,' Pete said. 'That's what counts.'

'That's what bloody worries me. He used to be so independent I felt proud of him. He reminded me of me. Not that I'd have told him, of course.'

'Perhaps you should.'

'When he took up teaching, which frankly I blame entirely on you, I thought he was off his head, but he really began to find his feet. Now he's back at square one with the tattooed tomcat.'

'I wouldn't worry. He's still young.'

Bill frowned.

'At his age I was already married, with a couple of kids and a business to run.'

'You're different. And the world has moved on.'

'Tell me about it!'

'I had another tooth out last week,' Bill said. 'Second this year, fuck it. You?'

Pete opened his mouth wide, then loudly clamped his jaws together.

'Still got all mine.'

To further annoy Bill, who had precious little left, Pete tugged at his full head of dark hair.

'Bugger all I can do about that. Baldness is hereditary. About the only bloody thing I did inherit. Otherwise, I'm a miracle of science. Every time I go through an airport I set bells ringing. Could be my new hip, or new knee. But that's the price for being a sporting icon.'

Pete smiled. All his life Bill had played a lot of ball games, though none very well. Fortunately, it had never stopped him enjoying them, or going on about them as if he was the greatest player in the world.

'A single condom will do it,' Pete said. 'I was once stopped at security and practically undressed before I discovered the offending article in my breast pocket. I always thought it would make a great opening for a whodunnit: how the wife discovers her husband's been unfaithful, that sort of thing.' Bill's brow furrowed.

'Personally, I never use them. For me it's the real thing or nothing.'

'So it's nothing, then?'

'Not for a bit, no.'

When Bill got up to go to the Gents, Pete started thinking of Andrea. Pete was the last person to wear his heart on his sleeve and had never been one to get things off his chest. Andrea was the only woman he had ever shared with Bill, and he wasn't at all proud of himself. He had introduced them soon after Carol's death, hoping she might distract him, and after overcoming his initial reluctance, Bill had fallen madly in love. In no time their engagement was announced, only for Andrea to then change her mind, ostensibly on discovering that Bill wasn't as well-off as she imagined. To pick his brains, she had invited Pete to lunch in a smart Chelsea bistro, after which they had spent the afternoon in bed, an explosive event in every respect, as from the moment he had woken from his post-coital snooze, Pete could remember nothing whatsoever about it. Outraged, Andrea had thrown him out, and soon afterwards got back together with Bill. Another wedding was planned, but once again she failed to show up. Since then she had not been seen or heard from by either man, while Pete was left with an uncomfortable secret he was terrified he might at any moment inadvertently disclose to Bill.

After two years, Bill had finally stopped talking about Andrea, and had settled into a sexless widowhood. Pete, on the other hand, free from his brief, disastrous marriage, had no intention of giving up the chase, though he would never have put it that way, insisting he could take it or leave it; even though, as Bill liked to chide him, he had never been able to leave it for very long.

'Heard about Andrea?' Bill said disconcertingly, when he returned to the table.

'Who, your Andrea?'

'Hardly mine.'

'Don't tell me she's found another husband?'

'How did you know?'

'Not exactly rocket science. Do you mind?'

'No. Yes. I don't know. She cost me a packet in cancellations. I still dream of all those lovely golf courses in Mauritius.'

'Take me instead.'

'Not bloody likely!'

Pete grinned.

'Who's she ensnared this time?'

'One of my old clients, as it happens. Rich as Croesus. Jammy bastard.'

'I don't envy him. You made a lucky escape. She'd have ruined your life.'

'What makes you think that?'

'Trust me,' Pete said, perilously close to giving the game away. 'She was the real deal.'

'There's nothing real about Andrea. She was so full of combustibles if you'd lit a match anywhere near her you'd have gone up in flames.'

'Sadly, I never got that close.'

4

Like many of his generation, Guy had done his fair share of drugs, but if asked to describe himself - something he'd never have done voluntarily – would most likely have said 'law abiding', not because he had any particular respect for authority or convention but because he didn't want to be bothered by the outside world. His internal world was cluttered enough, and quietly working with his hands to a prescribed routine, stilled the cacophony in his head and kept him level.

Guy had only ever been interested in the present, in extracting the most from any given moment. When something was finished - a piece of work or even a love affair – he instantly put it behind him. Alas, throughout his life other people had consistently refused to behave as he expected or hoped, and in trying to lead a simple, unencumbered life, he had created only chaos and disappointment. If it was true, as he maintained, that he had never broken a promise, that was only because he had never made one, allowing others to believe whatever they wished and to join up the dots for themselves. To the unasked question 'what did they expect?' the forsaken lover might have justifiably responded 'what did he expect?' Now approaching 70, it was a question Guy remained incapable of asking, let alone answering.

Far from having his head in the clouds, Guy saw quite clearly how Brexit might disrupt his peaceful life in France. But as usual he preferred not to worry about things he could do nothing about. Unlike Alice, his young Chinese wife, who having convinced herself beforehand that the UK would never turn its back on the EU as it had on Hong Kong, was now working herself into a frenzy over where and how they would live and where young Luke would one day go to school.

'Who cares?' Guy asked, irritated by the fuss she was making. But when she tried to explain, she could see he wasn't listening. Unlike Guy, who had grown up in comfort and lacked for nothing, her childhood had been spent in a tiny, overcrowded home in a world where political decisions made far away could have sudden, dramatic consequences for everyone; where living between the lines and maintaining any privacy – a concept for which in her own language no comparable word existed – was unimaginable. 'We'll stay where we are, and if necessary I'll teach Luke at home. In fact, I rather like the idea. In any case, that's all a long way off.'

'To you maybe, but I won't live with such uncertainty,' Alice said. 'Nor should Luke. What if we're not permitted to stay?

Or can't travel freely? Or no longer have access to cheap medical treatment? What happens when you get ill?' she added, drawing attention to the pronounced difference in their ages. Unlike those many Frenchmen who appeared to enjoy arguing hour after hour about nothing in particular, Guy was uninterested in sharing his opinions or hearing other peoples'. In 30 years he'd befriended none of his neighbours nor any of the locals, and had never been invited for a meal into anyone else's home, even by those he had employed for years and to whom he remained convinced he was just another Anglo-Saxon ripe for the plucking. To those expatriate Brits living in the region on dwindling pensions, who could no longer afford to return to the UK even if they wanted to, and were unsurprisingly anxious about their future status in a foreign country, Guy's passive approach would have seemed just as mystifying as it did to Alice. But having married primarily to get her a British passport, it seemed absurd to him that she should now be jumping up and down at the prospect of not being allowed to remain in a country she manifestly detested.

5

David Cameron's resignation immediately after the Referendum provoked mixed reactions at the golf club, where Bill had taken up pretty much permanent residence. Members who had rejoiced at the result, felt understandably angry with the PM for breaking his promise to see the process through. That his position might be untenable was not considered sufficient reason for failing to keep his word, yet no more than to be expected from a former ad man; an omen perhaps that the UK's departure from the EU might not be as simple or straightforward as supporters of Brexit, ever-keen to simplify complex issues and see things in black and white, had argued throughout their campaign. That there had been exaggeration and dishonesty on both sides was instantly forgotten by the millions who refused to accept the result, and who would over the coming years do everything possible to prevent the UK leaving the EU. The belief that the Referendum had been decided exclusively by elderly, provincial, ill-educated xenophobes, was widely held, particularly by those who could never imagine voting against their economic self-interest. But as in the earlier Referendum over Scottish independence, whose outcome had similarly confounded the pundits, the silent majority had wisely kept their counsel, regarding it as no one else's business how they cast their ballot.

On weekdays, Bill could usually be found after his morning round at the Members bar, holding forth on Brexit and sundry hobby horses, for which he had a captive audience, except among the bridge players, who found his hectoring tones distracting from their game.

'If you don't like it, there's a perfectly good card room upstairs.'

'Too bloody cold in there.'

'Not half as cold as it will be when EDF and the other Frog companies who own all our energy, decide to turn the gas off.'

'Why would they do that?'

'Why wouldn't they? They're Frogs, aren't they?'

To which, like so many remarks at that curious time, there appeared to be no answer.

Outside on the course the normally lush fairways were scarred by tractor tracks and earth movers, as tees were extended, greens enlarged, bunkers grassed over and trees which had stood for a hundred years felled in the specious cause of authenticity. Between the holes, among the wreckers' debris, huge piles of pristine logs stood ready to be sold off or stolen.

'Authenticity is bollocks,' Bill said. 'Golfers aren't indigenous and they aren't chopping us down.'

'First sensible idea we've heard,' came a voice from the card table.

'Technology has moved on.'

'We don't have any choice.'

'Not if we want to keep our juniors.'

'Why do we need them?'

'The course is too short.'

'Not for me.'

'Nor me.'

'Bloody kids.'

Three pairs of eyes followed Bill's as they moved along a row of photographs of former club captains hanging above the bar. When he reached his own, Bill raised his eyebrows, hoping for some acknowledgement from his earlier, more innocent self.

'I don't remember you standing up for the old farts when you were captain,' someone said, evidently reading Bill's mind.

'That's because he wasn't yet one.'

'He is now!'

'There were other issues,' Bill heard himself say. 'Bigger issues.'

'There always are.'

'There wasn't the time.'

'There never is.'

'Nor the money.'

'There is now.'

'Times have changed.'

'It's no longer the same.'

'It's always the same.'

'All for a few spotty kids.'

Over and over, day in day out, the same inconclusive arguments interrupted only by the closing of the club house, and Bill moving unsteadily towards the Gents and out into the lonely night.

## 6

'Dad wants me to move out,' Ivan told Pete, over a pint at the pub. 'He told me to my face. But move out where? And what about Mel? Where the fuck's she supposed to go? Has he said anything to you? He must have. He tells you everything.'

'Nothing specific,' Pete said, not sure how much to reveal. 'He's just letting off steam, the way he does when he's cross. He probably thinks it's time you stood on your own two feet. For your sake as much as his.'

'What for? There's bags of room here. Better me than a bunch of bloody strangers.' There'd been much talk lately of a 'bedroom' tax on owners of big houses.

'He'd never do that.'

'If this Fascist government gets its way he won't have any choice.'

'Sounds more like socialism to me,' Pete said. 'Anyway, that's not the point. At your age...'

'What's age got to do with it? On my salary I can't afford to buy anything, if that's what he thinks. No one can.'

'He doesn't expect that.'

'Well, what the fuck does he expect? It's my home as much as his.'

'I'm not sure he sees it that way.'

'Then it's time he bloody did.'


Ivan had always found his Godfather easy to talk to. Over the years, Pete had frequently acted as a conduit between father and son, sometimes responding to a direct appeal from Ivan, occasionally acting on his own initiative, once or twice at the behest of Carol, who felt too conflicted to function independently. The most Bill had ever asked of Pete was advice he'd no intention of taking, using his old friend as a sounding board for his own strong opinions. A phone call from Bill was an uncommon event, so when a couple of days earlier he had rung up after midnight, Pete had assumed bad news was on the way.

'What? Oh no, nothing like that,' Bill said. 'I'm just ticked off, properly ticked off. Know what the little shit's gone and done this time? Not content with accusing me of sacrificing his whole bloody generation on the altar of some nostalgic post-Imperial bullshit, he goes and announces on some bloody media shite to the whole effing world that he is now so ashamed to be called British that he intends to publicly burn his passport, as a so-called gesture of solidarity with our European bloody confreres. Well, good luck to him is all I can say. Let's see how far he gets without one. He might then find that the glorious old EU isn't quite as borderless as he imagines. As for the bank of mum and dad, there'll no longer be any effing dividends for young master Ivan. We'll also see how Tarantula Tits gets on, now I've binned all her vegan muck. I've stuffed the fridge with lots of lovely offal and game, anything I could think of to get up her little pierced snout.'

'Isn't that a bit childish?'

'Meeting fire with fire.'

'I'm sure Ivan doesn't mean anything by it.'

'Precisely my point. They bang on and on as if nothing they say or do has material consequences.'

'They feel powerless.'

'Powerless, my arse. They move in here as if they own the place, shift my stuff without asking, criticise everything I say and do, and expect to be thanked for it. Talk about the evils of colonialism, they're the biggest effing colonisers of all! They care only for their own convenience. They talk the talk but can they walk the walk? Can they fuck. Actually, that's all they do as far as I can tell, all day and bloody night by the sound of it.'

'You're just jealous.'

'Certainly not.'

'You can't stand to see them enjoying themselves.'

'You only have to look at their glum bloody faces to see they don't.'

'They still have their whole lives ahead of them.'

'A game of rugger on a wet Saturday afternoon, followed by an evening down the boozer,' Bill ruminated. 'We were jolly content with that. Now it's all 'elf and safety, and don't go out because it's drizzling and little Johnny might get his hair wet. Whose side are you on, anyway?'

'Nobody's.'

'I'll tell you what really gets up my nose. It's because for all their endless bloody education, top private schools and colleges and all the other overpriced rubbish, all of course paid for by muggins here, they've ended up knowing the square root of fuck-all, and being completely unprepared for the outside world. Not only do they not thank us, they can't stop telling us what a cushy time we had in comparison. If you happen to point out the small matter of all the wonderful scientific and technological advances they benefit from which never existed in our day, of having instant access to worlds of information we'd have spent our whole lives in libraries trying to research, they can't actually do anything for themselves. Remember when they put pocket calculators in schools and, duh, suddenly no one could do mental arithmetic? At least someone put a stop to that bloody nonsense. But ask them to change a plug and they say 'Fuck off. Call the electrician.'

'Is that it?'

'Yes. No. There's plenty more where that came from.'

'Bill, I've heard it all before.'

'Not from me.'

'Yes from you.'

'When?'

'All the time. You're like a broken record.'

'You might be a bit more sympathetic.'

'I am sympathetic. I'm just trying to see it from their angle too.'

'Well, don't.'


7


'I couldn't bear Ivan and the vegan assassin endlessly telling me where to go and what to do,' Bill said to Pete a few weeks later over lunch at the Fox & Grapes. 'But now the bugger's gone I rather miss him. In fact, it's made me realise the place is far too big for little old me, so I might as well bung it on the market before everything goes tits up. You don't happen to want to move back in?'

'I can't. I mean I'd love to, but I'd never get any work done. I used to think I was pretty disciplined but now spend all my time wondering where the world's going, and never achieve anything.'

'Maybe you've run out of things to say.'

'It isn't about having things to say.'

'Why not?'

'It's about hoping to find answers by asking the right questions.'

'Which are?'

Pete shrugged.

'If I knew that I wouldn't feel so effing useless.'

'Then you'll be having time for another jar,' Bill said, in an Irish accent, picking up their empty glasses. Pete nodded. 'Good man.'

25

'So who d'you think they'll get to replace Cameron?' Bill asked.

'What's the choice?'

'My money's on the big hairy blonde.'

'Who?'

'Boris Johnson, of course. I thought you were well-informed.'

'Life isn't just about politics.'

'The heir presumptive would disagree. He would tell you everything is political.'

'Yes, well. He'll grow out of that. We all did.'

'Personally, I no longer give a bugger. They're all a complete bloody shower. Couldn't organise the proverbial piss up. And you know why?' Bill paused, waiting for an answer he had no interest in hearing. 'It's because none of them have ever had a proper job. They think a bloody Think Tank is work, but that's all bollocks. They have no experience of what the real world is like, and what's more, they couldn't care less. I worked with people like that all the time, and they're all the effing same, doesn't matter which political stripe. Like Cameron, they just make it up as they go along.'

'Aren't you being a wee bit cynical?'

'Just realistic, old chum. None of them want to admit that we're a third-rate has-been of a country with fuck-all say in the world. We no longer make anything, and if anyone invents something clever, which in the past we were bloody good at, Johnny Foreigner snaps it up from under our noses. Or in the case of the Chinks, nicks it.'

'But we're meant to be one of the biggest economies in the world.'

'Only on paper. Take away the City and we're the size of a banana bloody republic.'

'I thought that's why you wanted us out of the EU. That's what you always said.'

'I did. Still do. Unfortunately, I no longer think it'll happen. There isn't the political will. Too much like hard work to a generation who've no idea what hard work is.'

'You don't seriously believe that?'

Bill shook his head.

'I know it.'


# 8


To Bill, the months following the Brexit Referendum felt like a phoney war in which everyone appeared convinced that as long as they did nothing, nothing could happen; one minute geared up for action, the next confronted with lassitude and inertia. He remained ever hopeful that so much hot air might generate something, he hardly cared what as long as it demonstrated that the voice of the individual still counted for something, and that Brexit could not now be overturned. Remainers claimed that the Leave campaign had broken the law and that the Government was now acting illegally. Leavers asserted that ministers and civil servants were deliberately sabotaging any constructive efforts to come to a meaningful deal; and that a Prime Minister who had once loudly proclaimed 'Brexit Means Brexit', was preparing to renege on her commitment and sell the UK down the river, treating voters like investors in a company who belatedly discover they own non-voting shares. What are the three most useless things in the world? Bill liked to joke: a minority share in a private company and the Pope's balls. Except that it was the majority who were now being told their votes didn't count by a succession of retired Prime Ministers who were acting as if they were still in office, insisting that the Referendum must now be re-run, as all earlier EU Referendums had been re-run which had failed to produce the required result. But that, as Bill insisted, was one thing up with which the Great British Public would never put; and even the dimmest politician must have sensed that a reluctance to play fair might not after all result in a triumph for 'common sense', but in an even larger majority for leaving Europe once and for all.

Ivan was not convinced by anything his father said, and nothing could change his mind: by 'stealing' his future, Bill's generation had forfeited the right to make political decisions on his behalf. Far from extending the franchise to sixteen-year-olds, as the Labour Party was now proposing, Bill mischievously suggested that no one under 40 should be given the vote; and if that was considered too radical, that the old University seats should at least be restored, so that Bill, among a few thousand other Oxbridge graduates, might have two votes. Britain was, after all, a property-owning democracy and Bill owned two properties.

'You're not serious,' Ivan said. 'You can't possibly believe that.'

'Actually, I do,' Bill said, putting on his poker face. 'It's not very long ago that you had to own property to vote, and women only got it in this country after the First World War. That's when the rot started. In France until 1945 a woman couldn't get a job or open a bank account without her husband's written permission, and there are still plenty of places where women aren't even permitted to drive. Just think of it, a world without women drivers!'

'I don't believe you. You made that up.'

'Google it. The trouble with your generation is, you don't know any history. You think life's always been like this, when the whole point is, it never was. If you want to go anywhere, you programme your sat nav. If you need a fact, you go online. I bet you don't know how to read a map or use a filing system or change a fuse, because you've never had to. You probably don't even know what a fuse is. But when all this technology suddenly packs up through some cyber attack or, more likely, a common or garden cock up, you'll be up shit creek without a paddle, unable to go anywhere or mend anything. By then all the Polish electricians will have gone back home, so you'll be well and truly fucked. Now tell me, is that what you really want?'

9

As an only child, Bill had been left to his own devices, and from an early age acquired the habits of self-reliance. Practical and capable, he had received little affection from his parents, and only by determination and hard work rather than any innate sense of self-worth, had he made a success of his professional life. That had all been carefully explained to him by Carol after she gave up her job in the City and turned to psychotherapy as a career. And if at times Bill found her jargon-filled explanations difficult to follow, he was nevertheless happy to feel that he was no longer alone, and that for once someone else was on his side. This had been reinforced by his determination to be a quite different parent to his own children; and if, unsurprisingly, it hadn't always come easily, he had made himself into the kind of father he believed he would have liked to have had, playing with the children when they were small, and regularly attending school plays and sports days, always encouraging and rarely critical, though if he felt they'd made a mistake or taken a wrong turning, he couldn't help speaking out. Of all human activities, being a parent cannot be taught, nor the results guaranteed, and if, as a result, he had provoked rebellion, that was only to be applauded. Bill had been especially wounded by his parents' refusal to attend his 60th birthday party in Puglia, all expenses paid, and when, not long afterwards, they had committed suicide together, his immediate reaction had been rage rather than sadness or remorse.

'You all right Dad?' Bill's elder daughter Millie was on the phone, calling from her home in Brighton. It was Sunday evening and he was in his den watching golf on TV.

'Sorry, darling. I'll call you straight back. The playoff's starting.'

'At this time of night?'

'From America.'

'Oh, right.'

Bill smiled at Millie's innocence. It reminded him of one of his favourite golf stories: of the young Sam Snead's incredulity on seeing his photograph in a New York newspaper when he'd never been there. Though he'd never have admitted to preferring any one of his children, Millie was Bill's favourite. Not as pretty as her younger sister or as bright as his son, she had always been a warm and loving presence, particularly after Carol's death, when she had left her husband to look after their two children while she took care of 'her dear old dad,' though Bill didn't much care for her use of the word 'old'.

'Won't be long,' Bill added. 'Sudden death.'

'Who's dead?' she said, immediately anxious.

'First to win a hole. Could be over any minute or go on for ages. You never know.'

'I suppose not.'

'A bit like life!'

That evening the playoff went on so long that Bill fell asleep, and when he woke up it was too late to call Millie back.

First thing in the morning she rang again.

'I'm OK,' Bill said. 'I promise. I nodded off in front of the box.'

'How much are you drinking?'

'Not a lot. Half a bottle, maybe. No more.'

'Wine or whisky?'

'Depends.'

'Every day?' Every meal, Bill thought, but said: 'More or less.'

'More *or* less?'

'It's bloody lonely here without your mother.'

'I know. But it won't be for long.'

'What do you mean?'

'Someone's bound to buy the house. Then you can move into town and be near all your clubs and things.'

'Oh yes, right.'

There was a lull in the conversation. It was half past ten in the morning. Bill poured himself a glass of Fino. Not his first.

'Dad?'

'Yes?'

'Ivan...'

'What about him.'

'He's worried about you.'

'No, he's not. He wishes I was dead. Me and the rest of my generation.'

'Not really.'

'Yes, really. He thinks when I'm gone he'll be quid's in and can live the life of Riley.'

'It's not easy being a teacher. He works very hard.'

'Not you too? When I was his age...'

'I know dad. You had tin bath in froont room and took a canary down t'mine in case of gas leak.'

'Very funny. Anyway, I thought he'd given up teaching.'

'He's tutoring some rich Russian kid trying to get into public school. But the brat won't lift a finger, so it's pretty hopeless.'

'What's wrong with the traditional brown envelope?'

'Honestly, Dad!'

'Is he still with that funny little thing with the tattoos?'

'You mean Melanie? As far as I know. You wouldn't guess it, but she comes from a very posh family. Title, family seat. All the trimmings.'

'You certainly wouldn't. Have you seen what she eats?'

'She's very good for Ivan, despite her appearance.'

'I'm glad someone has influence over him.'

'Who does he remind you of?'

'No one immediately springs to mind. Why?'

'He's just like you.'

'Bollocks.'

'I promise.'

'But he doesn't even play golf.'

'Is that some kind of test?'

'Certainly.'

'Then perhaps you should teach him.'

'He'd never listen.'

'Don't be so sure.'


## 10


'Fancy a game?' Pete asked Bill.

'When were you thinking?'

'Anytime, really. I'm not doing much.'

'Me neither.'

'See when you can get a tee time. Pull rank.'

'There's nothing deader than an ex-Captain, I promise you, but I'll try.'

'Good. I need to get out. If I hear one more argument over Brexit...'

On the second green, Bill said: 'You've been practising.'

'Not really.'

'Yes, really. I can tell. Taking lessons?'

Pete shook his head.

'Natural ability.'

'Bollocks!'

'Plus the odd video on You Tube.'

'Whatever it is seems to be working.'

'All fixes work for five minutes. Until the gorilla gets out of its cage.'

'Tell me about it. Not completing the backswing. Coming over the top...'

'Not releasing the clubhead or using the legs properly.'

'We're old men. What do you expect?'

'It's a skill I intend to master.'

'You never will. No one ever does. Even the top pros have full-time coaches to keep them on the fairway.'

'Have you noticed how whenever anyone reaches the top, they start buggering about with their swing? Not content with having beaten the best, they immediately want more,' Pete said. 'They're so insecure they become easy pickings for the snake oil salesmen, and then it's Goodnight Vienna.'

'It's the same with anything. When you get to the top you find it isn't that special after all, and everyone wants a piece of you. Look at Langer. Five minutes after winning the Masters he feels empty inside and discovers Jesus. You think fame is going to free you when in reality it does the opposite. These days everyone thinks they have a natural born right to celebrity, without doing anything to earn it. Thank God I never had any such ambition.'

'Didn't you?' Pete asked vaguely, lining up his putt.

'Not really. I wanted some of the better things in life but knew I'd have to earn them myself. Who doesn't? A nice house, decent cellar, enough lolly to send the kids to proper schools, a pretty wife. But I never wanted power over other people. I had enough trouble controlling myself.'

Pete pumped the air as his ball disappeared into the hole.

'Nice putt,' Bill said, genuinely pleased for Pete. 'Now what was it you wanted to talk about, because I'm bloody sure it wasn't golf.'

## 11

'That son of mine certainly gets around.' Bill said, as they sat on the veranda of the halfway house, drinking sherry and Bovril. 'Bloody good tipple this. Warms the old cockles.'

'Particularly on a day like this.'

'There won't be many more of these,' Bill said, squinting up at the cold winter sky.

'What a pair of old farts we've become.'

'I like being an old fart.'

'I don't.'

'No point fighting it.'

'Rage, rage against the dying of the light.'

'That's bloody good,' Bill said, glancing at Pete. 'Did you make that up?'

'Honestly Bill!'

Bill winked.

'Just teasing.'

For weeks the country had been basking in an Indian summer, but winter had suddenly arrived, and only a few days remained in the year when golfers could get in a full round after lunch. Bill always felt moved when he left the golf club in darkness, a mixture of sadness and nostalgia, though for what he wasn't sure. It was the sort of feeling he rather imagined romantic poets writing about.

'Mellow fruitfulness, and all that cobblers,' he added.

'What are you doing for Christmas?'

'Millie's asked me down but I'm not sure I'll go. Too many memories.'

'Bill, it's been four years.'

'Tell me about it.'

'Didn't you say something about dating on-line?'

Bill nodded.

'I thought I'd give it a go but then couldn't face it. Everyone seemed so desperate. Me included.'

'I thought you didn't care. I mean about getting your leg over.'

'I don't. It's the company I miss. I keep going through Carol's old albums. She always imagined us in old age, side by side on the sofa, looking through them and having a good giggle. But all I do is blub. I can't help it. I feel so pathetic.'

'It shows you have feelings,' Pete said.

'It's embarrassing.'

'I wish I could do that.'

'Do what?'

'Express emotion.'

'Golfers don't cry.'

'I know. They just lose their balls!'

'What did you mean when you said that?' Bill asked. 'About feelings.'

'Nothing really.'

'Come on. Man up.'

Pete shook his head.

'It's something I've never admitted, but in all the years since my parents died, I've never shed a tear for either of them. I find that really shameful. I weep like a baby in front of any old Hollywood slop, but when it comes to real emotions, I don't seem to have them.'

'You seemed cheerful enough when you chipped in on 5.'

'That's different. Anyway, it was a fluke.'

'It was still a birdie.'

'But I didn't feel responsible for it.'

'No one else was.'

Pete looked thoughtful.

'I suppose not.'

For a while they sat in silence. Then Bill said: 'You know who you sound like?' Pete shook his head. 'Guy.'

'I wish. He has so much talent and doesn't even know it.'

'Much better that way. Think what he'd be like if he did.'

Pete shrugged.

'I always knew you hated him.'

'Can't stand the bugger. Doesn't mean I don't admire him.'

'I had a letter from him the other day.'

'What's a letter?'

Pete grinned,

'He doesn't do email. He's thinking of coming back.'

'What on earth for? This place is done for. Kaput. The politicos will make bloody sure of that.'

'For God's sake, Bill. Can't you forget Brexit for five minutes? We've 9 holes to go and I'm going to kick your ass.'

'No bloody way,' Bill said, slowly getting to his feet.

## 12

Bill was standing in the corridor between changing room and bar, scrutinizing noticeboards, when he heard his name. As the voice was female, he assumed it wasn't meant for him. The golf club was full of Bills.

'Bill,' the voice repeated. A hand then touched his shoulder.

'Helen....' Bill blinked. 'St Joseph's...' Bill blinked again. 'The hospice...' Bill shook his head. 'Carol...'

'Oh, yes. Sorry,' he said, though he still couldn't place her.

'No reason to remember. Usually no one does. All part of the process.' She paused, then added: 'I didn't come to the funeral. I make it a policy not to.'

Bill raised his eyebrows. An aspect of the past was reluctantly coming into focus: Carol, the hospice, a kindly woman, not an employee or visitor but some kind of trained volunteer, he seemed to remember, to whom he had more reasons than he knew to feel grateful. After Carol's final course of chemo, she had decided to spend her last weeks at St Joseph's, where the quiet was a huge relief from the faffing of friends who wouldn't leave her alone and had filled the sick room with spurious bonhomie. Carol hated being fussed over but hadn't said anything because they so obviously meant well. But peace was what she needed, and what, for her final weeks, the hospice had generously provided. Bill had spent much of that terrible time at the golf club bar, and never appreciated that his exclusion was not about him.

'She found peace and reconciliation,' Helen said. 'She had a good death.'

'Is there such a thing?'

'Most certainly.'

Good for whom, Bill wondered, wishing she would go away and stop reminding him of what he was missing more each day.

'I'm here with a team from...' She mentioned the name of another golf club in the area with which Bill's had a long-standing rivalry. Something to do with the social distinction between tradesmen and professionals, Bill couldn't remember which, such differences having pretty much disappeared, along with seaside postcards and Soho strip clubs.

'Ah, the enemy,' Bill said, at last coming to life.

'It's just a friendly. Golf and bridge. 18 holes, then 18 hands. It's a long day. I was taking a breather.'

'I don't blame you.' Then, surprising himself, Bill added: 'I used to play bridge. At university. God, don't you hate the word uni? Easley Blackwood. Was that his name?'

'Spot on. A bit old-fashioned now, I'm afraid.'

'I bet. It's ages ago. Back in the mists of time.'

'It's Roman Key Card these days, along with transfers and weak twos. Much too fussy, if you ask me.'

'Almost half a century. I can hardly believe it.'

'About asking your partner rather than telling them.' Bill shook his head. 'You should try again. Keeps the little grey cells ticking over.'

'Too long in the tooth. Old dogs and new tricks.'

'Nonsense!'

He could tell it was meant kindly, that she wasn't as fearsome as she looked, and she wanted him to know it.

'I lost my husband two years ago. He was a member here. One of the enemy,' she added, smiling at Bill.

'Mislay his tag, did he? Slipped the lead?' She smiled again. 'Sorry. Don't know where that came from. Honestly.' Bill shook his head. 'Crass of me. Didn't mean it. Idiot,' he went on, slapping his forehead, though he knew very well where it came from: he hated being reminded of Carol.

She touched his arm. 'It's fine. I'm used to it. It's my job. At least it was.'

'What? Crassness?'

'People saying the wrong thing. Embarrassed to show their feelings. Comes with the territory.'

'Thanks,' Bill said, and he meant it.

'I better get back. They'll be wondering where I've got to. I was only dummy for one board.'

You're nobody's dummy, Bill thought, but a nice, kindly woman. Not at all unattractive either, though for all her bravado perhaps not very confident, dressing to conceal rather than enhance her somewhat fuller figure. Unless, of course, she no longer cared. Perish the thought.

'Don't forget those little grey cells. They need regular workouts. Especially at your advanced age.'

She touched his arm again; then, beaming, pushed open the door to the Ladies Lounge, releasing a burst of laughter which instantly reinforced Bill's isolation.

Before leaving the club that evening Helen stuck her head round the door to say goodbye to Bill, who went home feeling much more chipper than in ages, though furious with himself for having been too timid to ask her surname.


## 13


'Don't laugh, but I've met someone,' Bill told Pete.

'Why laugh? You deserve it. Who is she?'

'I don't know. I mean, I don't know her name.'

'Have you slept with her?'

'Of course not. What do you take me for?' Pete smirked.

'A *coup de foudre*, then? Like Dante and Beatrice. Berlioz and Harriet Smithson. Hobbs and Sutcliffe. Wenger and Vieira.'

'Possibly. Too early to tell.'

'Particularly if you don't know her name!'

'I can find out easily enough.'

'But you haven't.'

'No, not yet.'

'What are you waiting for.'

'That's what I keep asking myself.'


## 14


'I've met someone,' Bill told Millie, over the phone.

'Do you want to bring her for Christmas?'

'Certainly not.'

'Why?'

'Too complicated to go into now. You don't mind?'

'Why should I? I'm delighted. You need someone in your life. And you have to stop missing mum.'

'I can't help it.'

'I know, but it's been four years.'

'Tell me about it.'

'Tell me about her.'

'Not much to tell so far. You won't laugh, will you, but I don't even know her name.'

'Dad!'

'Sounds daft, I know, but I have a funny feeling.'

'Does she know? I mean, you have spoken to her?'

'Yes, I have spoken to her.'

'But you still don't know her name?'

'I know her first name, if that's any good.'

'It's a start!'

'Thanks, darling.'

'You will say if you change your mind? About Christmas?'

'Of course.'

'Just one thing, Dad.'

'What is it?'

'Promise me it isn't that awful Andrea again?'

'No, thank God. She's just married someone else.'

'That wouldn't stop her.'

'Helen isn't a bit like Andrea. I promise you that.'

Finding Helen's particulars posed no problem, but summoning up the courage to call her did. For Bill was already gazing far into the future, wondering what it might be like to sleep with a woman other than Carol, and whether he wanted all the trouble of getting involved again, of having a decrepit partner to look after or of even being one himself, all the while forgetting that he had once cared for a dying wife, at least as much as he had been allowed to; superimposing on his long married life with Carol a simplified picture, all flaws airbrushed out, against which he was bound to measure anyone new, and against whom no one could possibly measure up. In short, finding every possible reason not to do the one thing he knew he most wanted in life.

## 15

'She says she likes theatre,' Bill told Pete.

'That doesn't make her a bad person.'

'Art galleries, too.'

'Not such a good sign.'

'Why?

'Oh, you know. Kulchur...' Pete grinned.

'She also plays bridge. To county standard, I'm told.'

Pete shrugged, uncertain if this was a good or bad sign.

'Worst of all, she has a much lower handicap than me.'

'Then it's off before it's even begun?'

Bill shrugged.

'I'll certainly have to up my game.'

'Regard it as an incentive.'

'That's what I told her. And you know what, she didn't seem to mind.'

'Why should she? Not everyone's as competitive as you.'

'She is.'

'Perhaps she's just a natural. Like Guy.'

'Yes, maybe.'

'Children?'

'Nope. None of those. At least as far as I know. Thank God.'

'Has she met any of yours?'

'Not yet, no.'

'Then what are you worried about?'

'I'm not.'

'Oh yes you are.'

'Well, maybe a smidge...'


## 16


'Sarah's written to me. First time in two years. I can't believe it's gone so fast.'

'I thought that was all over.'

'It is.'

'But you're still not divorced?'

'As good as. There didn't seem much point spending money on lawyers.'

'Except that no one else will take you seriously.'

'Maybe I don't want anyone to take me seriously.'

'Everyone needs someone to take them seriously.'

'You're only saying that because you're in lurve.'

'I'm serious.'

'Precisely.'


Pete refilled their glasses.

'Well?' Bill asked.

'Well what?'

'Are you going to see her?'

'No idea. I suppose I might.'

'Do you think you should?'

'I don't deal in shoulds.'

'Then perhaps you shouldn't.'

'I'm very fond of her son. She says he's struggling at his new school.'

'Can't his father help?'

Pete shook his head.

'Sarah won't have anything to do with him.'

'So it's down to you again?'

Pete nodded.

'I suppose so. And I do have time on my hands.'


## 17


'You really are a dark horse,' Pete said, 'How on earth did you pull it off?'

'Nothing to it, old boy,' Bill said. 'I asked her to partner me in the invitational mixed foursomes and naturally she agreed. No honestly, I never expected it. She's a miles better player and loads of other blokes were falling over themselves to get her, but I nipped in first, and she was too well-mannered to say no. When I really want something I go for it hammer and tongs and won't take no for an answer. I don't know any other way. The funny thing is, she didn't even hesitate. Amazing when you think how bloody difficult foursomes is, two players and only one ball, and no apologising. She's bloody good, never put me in the poo, and when I did it to her she never complained. We got to the semis, and then suddenly she got nervous and stopped playing her natural game, and for once rather gratifyingly I was the one holding things together. We halved on the last hole when she missed a slippery four-footer, by which time it was too dark to carry on, so there has to be a re-match. She couldn't have been nicer, told me how well I'd played and blamed herself entirely. Before the game I still wasn't sure what I really thought of her. I knew I was attracted. Others may not see it. Frankly, I rather hope they don't. But she has something I've rarely seen before. Carol had it. A kind of innate liveliness, which is very endearing. I've always trusted first impressions, so I wasn't completely surprised, but it's always nice to have one's hunches confirmed. Afterwards, we went for a drink, and then dinner, and one thing led to another, and now we're walking out together like Darby and Joan. She's a bit older than me, of course, though she doesn't look it.'

'How much?' Bill tapped the side of his nose.

'Never ask a woman's age. Let's say just a wee bit. Sounds cheesy, I know. Unlike you, I've never felt confident with women, so it's come as something of a surprise. A very welcome one, mind you, after these last grim years...'

18

The decisive event precipitating Bill's midlife crisis had occurred when he and Carol where looking through photographs of Bill's 60th birthday party, and Bill had failed to recognise a highly unflattering photograph of himself. So appalled had he been by this mysterious 'fat bastard', as Bill referred to the man he took to be an unknown gate-crasher, that he vowed on the spot to transform his life. A crash diet was accompanied by a hair-raising variety of barely credible new-age beliefs, and a fitness regime which had left him looking like a rag doll.

Bill never did anything by halves, and it wasn't long before Carol's concern for her husband morphed into a feeling that she was living with a stranger; and more worrying still, that were her old Bill ever to return, she might not want him. In the end, Carol's cancer and Bill's sense of responsibility brought them together for what had been perhaps the happiest period of their lives, though both now felt a certain wariness at the greater attention each was receiving from the other, constraint entering what for almost 30 years had been a pretty laissez-faire arrangement of two freewheeling personalities, though not one in which either had actually strayed very far, fantasies about other people somehow remaining just that, though Carol had once come perilously close in the car park of her local pub when, feeling lonely – Bill was then briefly living on his own – she'd made a drunken pass at Pete. Carol had subsequently overstated the extent of Pete's rejection as much as he made light of it. But if he quickly forgot, she never did, and for the rest of her life nursed a resentment which would never be satisfied until Pete and Sarah's marriage, which she considered her brainchild, had completely broken down. Neither Pete nor Sarah had been aware of the many and subtle ways Carol sought to undermine them, and it was only at the wake following her funeral that they discovered what she had done. Reluctant to believe that in her right mind Carol could ever have acted with such malevolence, both chose to blame it on her illness. But by then the damage was done, Pete and Sarah's brief reconciliation foundering, thanks to Carol's ghost, on Sarah's refusal to believe he could ever be trusted, an ironic outcome given that Sarah was the first woman to whom Pete had ever been faithful; since when, though not divorced, neither had felt quite up to restoring contact, self-preservation trumping self-realisation, as Bill during his New Age phase might have put it; and though during those four years both had had affairs, their less than satisfactory outcomes seemed to suggest that whether or not they liked it, their hearts might indeed be elsewhere.

'OK, what did she say?' Bill asked, when Pete told him he had failed to take his advice and had telephoned Sarah.

'Not much. She sounded surprised. Perhaps I wasn't acting as expected, though she never said what that was.'

'On a fishing expedition, I expect.'

Bill had never liked Sarah. To him, she was yet one more humourless cow who had come between him and his wife when she was dying, and was now threatening to come between him and his oldest friend.

'Not much to catch, if I'm what she's after.'

'You don't still support her?'

'I can barely support myself.'

'Thank God for that.'

'If I happen to have a bit over I try to help out. She's living in the middle of nowhere, and needs a car to get anywhere.'

'Hardly your responsibility.'

'I sort of feel it is.'

'Then sort of get over it.'

'It isn't that easy. She only has to mention Jack.'

'You're not his father.'

'Someone has to be.'

'Why you?'

'Because I want to be.'

'I see,' Bill said, taken aback. 'Well, of course, that changes everything.'

'Actually, I'm not sure it does.'

'How do you mean?'

'I'm either all in or nothing.'

'And?'

Pete shook his head.

'I haven't a clue.'


19


'Guy's decided to stay in France.'

'Typical.'

'I don't blame him.'

'Frankly, neither do I.'


20


'How was Mauritius?'

'Breathtaking. Best holiday of my life.'

'What did you do?'

'Absolutely fuck all.'

Pete smiled.

'That good, huh?'

'Better than I could ever have imagined. She's a dark horse, my Helen, when she gets her kit off. Very fit for a woman her age.'

'No time for golf then?'

'Only once a day, as the actress said. There are some lovely courses, provided you don't get stuck behind effing Krauts. They take forever and insist on putting out on every green. Some rounds I lost the will to live.'

'No doubt Helen revived you.'

'Indeed she did!'


## 21


Historians will one day look back on that strange, slack period of English history between 2016 and 2019, when for all the sound and fury, the protest marches and public demonstrations, the political speeches and high-profile law suits, the families and generations torn apart by opposing opinions and alternative visions of both past and future, nothing actually happened. The UK was not after all leaving the EU, but nor was she staying; and even if, at some unspecified point in the future, she did finally depart, she would not actually be going anywhere, but, as she had done throughout her long history, perch uncomfortably on the edge of Europe, an island yet not an island, in and yet not in, out yet not quite out, stiff necked from trying to face in different directions simultaneously.

Some would remember it as a time of reflection, when people came to their senses, whatever those were, when a government ostensibly committed to one course of action appeared to be following another, until quite suddenly, after two general elections, neither of which had produced the expected result, a bumptious new leader, to some a hero, to others a buffoon, would rouse the nation from its torpor. Like Boris Johnson or loathe him, at last it seemed that something would be done. Or not.

## 22

'He's a total fraud. You can't believe a word he says,' Pete told Bill.

'Oh, I don't know.'

'I do.'

'Women love him.'

'They always love shits.'

'You should know! At least he's alive,' Bill said.

'Strong personality, weak character.'

'Spot on. Did you just make it up?'

'I wish. An old girlfriend once said it of me.'

'Clever girl.'

'Used to winging it, even when he doesn't need to.'

'He's a journalist.'

'Better than another ad man. Or lawyer.'

'Oh, I don't know.'

'Did I tell you Guy's changed his mind again?' Pete said.

'No surprise there.'

'I don't blame him.'

'I blame the lot of them. Politicians. Journalists. Lawyers. The old. The young. The BBC. Everyone.'

'For what?'

'For everything.'

'You sound just like Ivan.'


## 23


Is there a point in life, Pete wondered, when people become unmistakeably themselves? A eureka moment or, more likely, a remorseless process of distillation by which, drip by drip, new experiences modify old ones, and the unhelpful are shed like so much dead skin? And if so, are we aware of it? Or do people only see themselves through the prism of others, measured by their possessions, or by the impact of work or love?

After almost 60 years, Pete still wasn't sure which was the real Bill: the jovial glutton and generous host, passionate games player, opinionated cynic, teller of bad jokes; the indulgent father, faux-philistine, patriotic flag-waver, successful ad man? Or Bill Mark 2, reborn at 60, the lean, austere evangelist for healthy living, suspicious of all orthodoxies yet intolerant of other opinions, forever pointing out every thing that was wrong with the modern world? Or some amalgam of the two, no longer appallingly judgmental, but also not quite his former, complacent conservative self: Bill-lite as it were, neither full cream nor fat-free, in which traits of an earlier personality still twitched like phantom limbs?

'Brexit'll either happen or it won't, and nothing you or I think will make a damn bit of difference,' Pete told Bill.

'I can't believe you don't care. Doesn't it bother you at all?'

'I've given up watching the news. As long as I'm free to get on with my life, I'm happy.'

'Isn't that rather selfish?'

'Probably. But better that than wasting my few remaining years on things I can do nothing about. Whether we're in the EU or out, tied to America's apron strings or run by unaccountable multinationals, the best I can hope for is to carry on ploughing my own little furrow. *Il faut cultiver mon jardin*, as the Frog philosopher said. My fur-lined rut. I'm not saying nothing else matters. Whatever we end up with will have good and bad aspects, but unless you mean to shoot the lot of them, you're far better off trying to improve your handicap. Like the proverbial sausage machine they used to bang on about at school, you'll at least see where all your energy is going. What does Helen think?'

'She doesn't like to talk about it. She's a peacemaker, so by nature a Remainer. If she has any strong opinions, she keeps them to herself. I often see her rolling her eyes just as I'm getting into my stride, so I've learned when to stop.'

'That's a first. I must congratulate her.'

'She may not look it, but she's bloody clever. Knows exactly when to speak up and when to keep stum. Plays me like a Stradivarius.'

'More like a clapped-out Joanna.'

'Touché.'

'The great thing is, you don't seem to mind. When you were with Carol...' Bill frowned.

'Don't remind me. Life felt like one long bloody examination.'

'Not all the time.'

'No, not always.'

'You seem much more comfortable in your skin these days.'

'Flabby though it is. I would never knock Carol. She was marvellous in many respects but she was never that easy to live with.'

'I can imagine.'

'And Helen is, well, just Helen. Honestly, I feel blessed.'

'Except when Brexit rears its ugly head.'

'Indeed. And even that, I keep telling myself, can't go on forever.'

'Don't be so sure.'


## 24

After leaving Cambridge, Guy had lost touch with his family. Despite the heavy Iron Curtain, the planet in those days felt a more accessible place, and countries later off-limits were relatively easy to explore. Happiest when travelling light, blessed with a robust physique and iron constitution, Guy had taken advantage of his new-found freedom, hiking fearlessly through North and South America, the Middle East and India, then working his passage south to Australia and New Zealand. Oblivious of events in the wider world, he had taken a succession of menial jobs his father would doubtless have considered a deplorable waste of a first-class brain and expensive education, the very things Guy was trying to escape. Using his hands, whether washing dishes or roping horses, seemed infinitely more fulfilling than writing essays at a library desk, regurgitating other people's ideas and pretending they were his own. Experiencing different cultures would, Guy imagined, clarify something for him. But for all his restlessness, he was not impatient, and while still in his twenties happy to go with the flow.

He'd promised to tell his sister wherever he was staying, and it was a telegram from her, after eight years away, that informed him of his father's unexpected death. Guy was in Australia, working on a ranch in the Blue Mountains, and saw no point going home. But within a year, to everyone's astonishment, he was back in England, working in the family business, manufacturing ladies' tights in the Midlands.

Other than his physique, he had little to show for his years of rough travel: the opening chapter of a picaresque novel, a few mawkish poems he would never re-read, some rolls of undeveloped film. He had kept no journal or diary, nor even picked up a pencil since walking out of life-drawing in Cambridge. Then one day, wandering through the Campo in Siena on holiday from the factory, he stopped to watch a young woman painting. Every so often she turned her head and smiled shyly. She wasn't very good, yet he was touched by her hopelessness. She seemed to be appealing to him but he hardly knew where to start. The faults in her picture were so glaring, she surely must have seen them for herself.

Suddenly, she got up and walked away, leaving everything behind. Assuming she'd gone for a pee, Guy stood guard over her easel and satchel. Then he sat down and started to re-work her picture. When at last she returned, ice cream in hand, and saw what he had done, she was furious. It was a lesson Guy would take decades to learn: the inability of the artist to always see what he is doing; a tactful way of telling the truth; the subjectivity of the work itself. That afternoon he bought hot-pressed paper and coloured pencils. Though he did not know it, he had at last found his metier, and hardly minded that he never saw the girl again.

Back in England he resigned his job, recommissioned his old Triumph, and hit the road. Everywhere he stopped he drew obsessively, in cafés and town squares, bus stations and bars, but always people, people, people.

Other than his sister, there was no one he could talk to. Homely and maternal, she seemed instinctively to understand him, divining his moods, encouraging his aspirations, never criticising him for coldness or casualness, for the way he drifted in and out of peoples' lives, unconcerned with the impression he made or the hurt he inflicted.

Accidentally caught up in a violent demonstration against American missiles in Europe, he met a German photojournalist, and for a while they travelled together. Talk of co-authoring a book of reportage came to nothing. For all his disdain for convention, when Gisela became pregnant Guy offered to marry her and she accepted. For a while they rented a flat on the Left Bank in Paris, but her work and his restlessness ensured they spent less and less time together, and for much of her childhood Guy saw little of his daughter

Dora. When, in her late-teens, they began to know each other, it felt to him as if she had instantly leapt from infancy to womanhood, so entranced was Guy by her sudden maturity and beauty.

For years he had hardly thought of the tower in Gascony. Then, from nowhere, it came to obsess him. Luckily, the owner had recently died and his daughter, living in Toulouse, had no interest in keeping it. More important, there were no other heirs to confuse the issue. To the locals, the ruin was an eyesore, and as long as Guy wasn't interested in the surrounding farmland, he could have it for next to nothing, which was a good thing as his father had left him precisely that.

Fortunately for Guy, his mother was more generous. Caught between two men she had both loved and understood, she had said little and done less. As a widow, she came into her own, revealing aspects of her character long suppressed. Not for her the gabble of fellow widows at bridge club or coffee house, but concerts and art galleries and educational cruises, often in the company of Guy's beautiful, talented daughter. Dora played the cello and sang like an angel, her grandmother insisted she must take her gifts seriously – unlike, she seemed to imply, Dora's once-precocious father, who had so little to show for his life. But that was not true. Guy had done a great deal, as his sister well knew and his daughter no doubt hoped. As for Guy, he could never understand why what he did concerned anyone else, or why they should even care.

'You never told me how you and Guy met up again,' Bill said. 'How you became such great mates.'

'Didn't I?' Pete said, feigning innocence.

'You knew I was looking for him, yet you never said a bloody word, you bugger.'

'I don't honestly remember.'

'Like hell!'

Pete shrugged.

'Perhaps I didn't think it was important. Just another of your fancies which you'd soon get over.'

'Mightn't I have been a better judge of that?' Bill suggested.

'I was right all the same. It wasn't Guy you were looking for, but your old self.'

'I wasn't in a great place, as you well knew.'

'You were mad as a hatter. But you're fine now, which is what matters. It's not as if I planned any of it. Guy just turned up at the art school and asked to join my class. I didn't even know it was him, he looked so bloody ancient. And he was going by a different name. I never meant to piss you off, but anyone could see he'd been through a lot and the last thing he wanted was to be reminded of all that dead stuff.' Bill nodded. 'You didn't really mind, did you?'

'What makes you think that?'

'Just a hunch.'

'Maybe not,' Bill said, after a long pause, then cocked his chin towards the bar. 'One for the road?'

'Won't Helen be wondering where you are?'

'She never asks, the darling.'

'You really have fallen with your arse in the butter, haven't you?' Bill grinned.

'Haven't I just!'

## 26

Shortly before his 60th birthday, Bill had become obsessed with finding Guy. At Cambridge they'd been in the same college, but for all that Guy was the object of widespread adoration he had discouraged intimacy, and when he failed to return for their second year, no one had bothered to find out why. Colourful rumours, perhaps unsurprisingly, made an appearance and then died away: that he'd been killed in a remote climbing accident or by some exotic bug; that he'd topped himself or even been bumped off over a woman or possibly a man – since when no one had ever put the record straight: Guy, because it suited him to vanish: his family out of shame and a belief that it was no one else's business. Now, for some reason Bill could never properly explain, even to himself, he needed Guy to be alive, somewhere, anywhere, on Planet Earth, so convinced himself it must be true. Why otherwise would it have occurred to him to look for someone he hadn't thought of in decades? No, Bill was convinced an unmistakeable message was being sent, as it turned out via his old friend Pete, that was all there was to it. And when at Pete's wedding the two men met again, all of the old magic had thankfully worn off. The Guy Bill now saw, dressed in a tatty tweed jacket and knitted tie, his long grey hair tied back in a pigtail, bore no resemblance to the young Adonis who had

once broken so many hearts, Bill's included. Yet for all his relief, Bill had to concede that this unfamiliar Guy seemed quite
at home in his now-wrinkled skin, while still giving little of
himself away and asking less of others. And when, not long
afterwards, he became an overnight sensation through a sell-
out show of his prints arranged by Pete, Bill was not in the
least surprised. He had always believed that Guy would do
something spectacular, even if he would never understand
how anyone could find so much variety in an assortment of
toilet rolls, or why one rich individual could possibly want to
own so many of them.


## 27


'Ivan, it's dad.'

'I know. Your number comes up on my phone.'

'Oh, right.'

'What is it? I'm rather busy.'

'With what, out of interest?'

'Reports. Marking. Next year's syllabus. The teacher's
happy lot. So if it's not important...'

'Not that important. I was wondering how you are.'

'I'm fine.'

'Mel?'

'She's OK.'

'Need anything?'

'No, nothing. Dad, I've really got to go.'

'Ivan?'

'What?'

'I want you to meet Helen. And she very much wants to meet you.'

'What for?'

'Why do you think? It's been six months without a dickie bird.'

'What did you expect when you chucked me out?'

'Hardly. I suggested for your own good you should find a place of your own. I even offered to pay the deposit. But perhaps you've forgotten.'

'I haven't.'

'At your age...'

'Don't go on. It was different in your day.'

'In what ways, may I ask?'

'Your generation had it so much easier.'

'Naturally we did. And our parents had it even easier than us, and their parents before them, going all the way back to the stone age. That's if you conveniently forget two world wars, the Spanish flu, Polio, TB, the concentration camps, the Great Depression, the ever-present threat of nuclear war between Russia and the USA. That's just for starters. We also had no money, no computers, no credit. We couldn't spend more than we earned or take money abroad. If you went bankrupt you were totally fucked. These days anything goes. You can get away with murder, no stigma attached. In fact, you're weird if you're not seriously weird. You lecture us about how awful life is, what with climate change and species dying out and the likelihood of a meteorite smashing into us and destroying everything. But at least we knew how to enjoy ourselves, and if things went wrong how to mend them. You have everything on a plate yet are miserable the whole bloody time.'

'Finished?'

'I could go on.'

'Don't bother,' Ivan said, hanging up.


'What did he want?' Mel asked, not sure it was a good idea talking to Ivan so soon after he'd spoken to his father.

'Nothing. Just the usual lecture about how fortunate I am compared to him. You'd think he'd spent his entire childhood up a chimney, with straw on the streets to dull the sound of coffins being wheeled away.'

'It's not like him to call.'

'He wants me to meet his new concubine.'

'He wants your approval.'

'Well, he's not getting it.'

'Ivan, your mum's been dead for five years. Isn't it time to let go?'

'Why does he need it? It's not as if he's ever cared what I think.'

'At least meet him half way.'

'What for?'

'To make life easier?'

'For him, you mean.'

'For all of us. You don't know what a pain it is having you like this the whole time.'

'Why are you taking his side?'

'I'm not, but this doesn't help anyone. It just poisons the well.'

'You don't even like him.'

'It's not about me.'

'Then why do you care?'

'For God's sake, Ivan. Grow up.'

## 28

'I can't believe Mel's taking dad's side,' Ivan told Pete.

'She isn't really. She's just trying to make peace. It's what women do. Some, anyway.'

'How can she? He voted for Brexit.'

'So did half the population.'

'They don't count.'

## 29

Borrowing Bill's car, Pete drove down to Dorset to visit Sarah and Jack. Ever since their separation three years before, he'd been living in limbo, married but not married, available yet unavailable. Without a job, he'd had too much time to brood and, nearing 70, felt he'd little to show for his life. Apart from Guy, he saw nothing of his old pupils, and any decent work he'd once done might have been by a stranger. Bill and Guy, his exact contemporaries, seemed to have found something in later life which had eluded him, and only a lack of envy stopped him feeling sorry for himself. Still reasonably fit, he felt younger than his years; and like others he spoke to, looked at the world with the eyes of a much younger man. Only when he passed a mirror, or became aware that someone – usually a woman – was paying him no attention, did he admit that something had gone, and he was getting old.

'You look good,' Sarah said straightaway, when they met in her village pub. 'Something must be going right.' Pete shrugged. 'You can tell me. We're friends now.'

Hardly, Pete thought.

'I cycle a lot. Probably drink too much.'

'Pulling the birds?' It was such an odd remark from Sarah, that he felt lost for words. To cover his evident embarrassment, she asked: 'Any work?'

'Only my own, and not much of that. It doesn't sell, if that's what you're asking.'

'That's a shame. You're really good.'

'Not compared to Guy.' Sarah shrugged.

'Perhaps it means more to him.'

'Perhaps,' he echoed. 'You?'

'I'm OK. Just about. It's Jack I worry about.'

'So you said.'

'The wrong sort of friends. Rude to me the whole time. We should never have left London.'

That was your decision, Pete thought: you never even asked my opinion. But then, you never did.

'It's a phase. He'll grow out of it.'

'It's still painful.'

'I can imagine.'

'He needs a father.'

'Doesn't everyone?' Pete's father, whom he'd hardly known, had died of a heart attack in his mid 40's. 'Why not come back to London?'

'Is that an invitation?'

'A suggestion.'

'I can't afford to. I should never have sold my flat. Once you're out of the London property market there's no way back in. It stinks, but that's how it is.'

64

'I wouldn't know.' Pete had never owned a home of his own, nor wanted to.

'No.' She put down her glass. 'Pete?'

'What is it?'

'Nothing.'

'Tell me.'

'I've thought a lot about what happened. I know it wasn't all your fault. I don't blame you, is what I'm trying to say.'

I've always known that, Pete thought, but chose to say nothing.

Immediately after lunch, he told Sarah he needed to get back and wouldn't have time to see Jack. She tried to persuade him to stay but he was resolute. Half an hour into his journey, somewhere near Stonehenge, he pulled into a lay-by on the A303 and burst into tears.

## 30

'Bill, I need another favour.'

'What now?'

'I wouldn't ask if it wasn't important.'

'I know that.'

'It isn't really for me.'

'No need to explain.'

'I feel I should.'

'Explain away then.'

'It's Sarah. And Jack.' Bill nodded. Pete was obviously in a state about something but, unusually for Bill, who liked to make light of serious matters, he had been reluctant to ask.

'They need my help.'

'How much?'

'How did you know it was money?'

'Isn't it always?' Pete shrugged. 'What's it for?'

'Somewhere to live. Just for a bit. While she, while we, try to sort something out. She sold her flat and can't afford to move back. I've never been in a situation like this. I feel so inadequate.'

'Hardly.' Bill put an arm around his old friend's shoulder.

'I knew I could count on you,' Pete said, forcing a smile.


31


Since parting from Sarah, Pete had moved around London, staying in Wimbledon with Bill, then house-sitting Guy's small studio. Paying a nominal rent plus outgoings, he had enjoyed his two years in that austere, uncluttered space, until recently a council flat with an outside iron staircase and small communal garden, close to the Houses of Parliament. Deserted at weekends, the historic neighbourhood greatly appealed to Pete, who liked to walk a lot. Just over the river, in a quiet leafy square not far from the art school, was a congenial pub with no piped music or video games, where regulars kept to themselves and Pete could drink his pint in peace. The possibility of Guy returning to England in the wake of the Referendum now galvanised Pete, who began to look for a place of his own. But whatever picture formed in his mind, it had no room for Sarah and Jack, and there was little prospect of his ever affording anything larger.

Then, out of the blue, the art school offered Pete back his old job. For all that the timing was miraculous, it nevertheless felt like a retrograde step. The appeal of contemporary art to students with little formal training was obvious, but their complacency and lack of curiosity, especially about the past, disturbed him. Though retired for only a couple of years, he wondered whether anyone would listen to him, and if what he had to say would be considered remotely relevant. Unable to make up his mind, he decided to ask the advice of someone in the know.

'Ah, a blast from the past,' Ivan said sarcastically, when they met at a pub near Ivan's school.

'It hasn't been that long. You make me feel a hundred.'

'I assumed you'd taken dad's side.'

'You know I never take sides.'

'Sorry.'

'How are things?'

'So-so.'

'Still with Mel?'

'Just about.'

'I like her. She's got spirit.'

'Bit of a whack job, if you must know.'

'Everyone should have a whack job once in their lives.' Pete said. The two men grinned at each other.

'Seen anything of the old bugger?' Ivan asked.

'All the time. He misses you.'

'I doubt it, now he's got his new tart.'

'Helen's hardly that.'

'She's not mum.'

'True, but you mustn't let it eat you up.'

'I can't help it.'

'He's happy. That's the important thing.'

'Is it? What about me? Doesn't my happiness count too?'

'That, I'm afraid, is your problem.'

'He doesn't help.'

'He can't.'

'Why the hell not?'

'Because no one can. That's what being grown up means.'

'He isn't. Most of the time he behaves like a spoiled brat.'

'In some ways he's surprisingly grown up. I promise you.'

'Then he should understand what I'm going through.'

'Believe me, he does.'

To change the subject, Pete asked about Ivan's school, then mentioned the job he'd been offered.

'Think I should take it?'

'Why ask me?'

'I thought you might know if anything I have to say is remotely relevant to them. I've hardly been out of teaching yet already feel like a dinosaur.'

'Don't worry about that. You always have something interesting to say.'

'Really? Do you think so?' Ivan smiled for the first time.

'I know it.'

## 32

Guy was almost back at the town square when he lost his footing. The unlit path was steep but there was no excuse for falling over. He hadn't drunk anything; the cobblestones appeared dry; and although there was no street lighting, he could easily see where he was going. Lying on the ground he could hear loud music and laughter from only a few yards away, but had no wish to re-join the party. As long as he lay there no one would notice him. It felt oddly satisfying, knowing no one would ask where he'd gone – Alice because she didn't speak the language, Luke because he would be riding one of the dodgems – nor why he still hadn't returned. They were used to him wandering off.

He could move his hands, feet and head, and was pretty sure nothing was broken. He just didn't feel like going anywhere. The very last thing he wanted was to return to the table and have to be sociable, the only sober adult among over 200 revellers, the only Englishman with no interest in Brexit or the *Gilets Jaunes* or anything else which seemed so important at that time to everyone in the world but him.

To Guy, each year was much the same: every summer he went to the local fête with the best of intentions, wanting to appear friendly towards people he'd known by sight for decades, people who knew far more about him than he ever would about them, to prove he wasn't like any of the others: not another supercilious foreigner who couldn't be bothered to learn the language; a retired accountant in a beret drinking pastis at 11am, and playing endless boule or skittles with the locals; one more con-man who, having insinuated himself into the community, would do a midnight flit owing thousands to everyone, bringing obloquy onto the whole expat community. Yes, it was all reassuringly familiar: the same food, the same people, the same band; the same jokes; the exact same routine; the one evening in the year when everyone automatically got together, no one asked why, an utterly familiar ritual subsidised by the commune to which many gave their time for free because that was what you did when you belonged – which Guy was the first to admit he had never tried to do, while also maintaining that hardest of relationships, between employer and employed: friendliness without familiarity, where favours were readily exchanged but certain boundaries never safely crossed.

When Guy had moved to Gascony, the summer fête had gone on for a week, ending in a parade of floral floats topped by waving children, a concourse of vintage cars and a nocturnal ramble through the moonlit countryside to the ruins of a Roman villa, followed by onion soup for all back in the town square. Now there remained only a few unconnected events spread over the summer months: a bogus medieval fair, an outdoor snail-fest, an afternoon of bull jumping in the village stadium. But if over the decades this annual festival, like so much else, had been trimmed down, the dedicated fête-shist, as Guy disparagingly referred to them, might still spend all of July and August moving from village to village, town to town, filling his nights and his stomach with much the same food – duck, paella, duck, wild boar, duck, snails and yet more duck, interwoven with terrine, melon and floc (the local aperitif), croustade (the local apple tart) and Armagnac (the local digestif), plus a hard piece of camembert from the other end of France, whose surprise appearance no one had ever been able to satisfactorily explain.

Guy pulled himself into a sitting position and took out his tin of roll ups. Uninterested in the impression he made, after so many years he knew, or at least imagined he knew, what local people thought of him. To the French he was a typically eccentric Englishman, obviously wealthy because no one but a rich man would dress so poorly or drive such a broken-down car, who lived, as they imagined such people must do in England, in a kind of grandiose squalor in his medieval tower. To the English expats he was far more suspect because none could precisely place him: keeping too much to himself and showing no interest in their activities, with an unforthcoming Chinese wife, and a young son at the village school who spoke perfect French with no trace of an accent – unlike Guy who, though fluent, always sounded as if he hardly understood a word he was saying.

Sitting on the ground, insulated from the noisy crowd, the bright lights and loud music, Guy felt calm for the first time that evening. He wasn't sure what had been worse, Alice's endless badgering or the insistent finger-jabbing of an overbearing expat who seemed to hold Guy personally responsible for the Brexit debacle. Guy had refused to argue with the man, or with his wife when she joined in, because he didn't care a damn what happened to them. He had as much to lose as anyone, and like everyone else, had to suck it up. If things hadn't gone to plan, that was no one's fault, it was just the way life was: that the pound, like interest rates, had gone down rather than up; that houses weren't selling; that local protests against the government in Paris and globalisation generally were causing massive inconvenience to everyone, was something they all had to live with. Even his own sister, to whom he was much attached though they hardly saw each other, had applied for German nationality to secure continued EU membership, a move Guy found incomprehensible in the light of their father's experience under the Nazis; something which Guy, who never wished to live anywhere else, could never have brought himself to do. But as in so many things, he found himself in a minority. Which was just one more reason to keep his opinions, like his feelings, to himself.

Stubbing his rollup out on the cobblestone, Guy glanced at his watch and saw the face was smashed. Getting slowly to his feet, he noticed a trail of pee running down the cobblestones, and wondered if he had wet himself after his fall; then saw it had started somewhere else and that it was that which had caused him to slip. One hand pressed against the church, he took a couple of hesitant steps, found he could walk unaided, and gingerly made his way back to his table, just as a couple of teenagers, holding between them a huge black bag, moved between the long trestle tables, collecting up the scraps: duck bones, discarded bread, chips, empty bottles, paper plates, plastic beakers, while replacing them with new plates and re-filled carafes, a seamless, coordinated routine which in all those years Guy had never tired of watching.

'I was worried,' Alice said, when Guy sat down beside her and lifted his son onto his knee.

'Obviously not that worried.'

'Where have you been?'

'If I didn't know better, I'd think you were jealous,' Guy said, playing with Luke's hair.

'You look a mess.'

'Do I?'

'Yes, Daddy, you do,' Luke said.

'Well, maybe I am. The truth is, I slipped and fell on my way back from the Gents.'

'Daddy, why don't you pee in the street, like everyone else.'

'Because I'm not a bloody frog,' Guy said. It was not a term he could ever remember using, even though he had no doubt thought it many times.

'Yes, why don't you?' Alice echoed.

Guy began to feel dizzy, perhaps from the fall, more likely from the bright lights and the insistent thrumming of loud speakers which would continue until dawn and still be heard from the tower two kilometres away.

'Shall we go home?' Guy suggested.

'Sure,' Alice said, ever ready to escape any contact with the locals. 'Let's go.'

'Must we, Daddy? I want another ride on the dodgems. With you.'

'I didn't mean this very minute.'

Then why suggest it? Alice wondered, sitting down again.

It was after midnight when they finally got home, Guy carrying Luke most of the way on his shoulders. Guy then went straight to bed and slept for twelve hours, unaware that Alice wasn't beside him, and for the next few days they barely spoke, moving around each other like suspicious animals.

When a phone call from his sister the following week told Guy of their mother's death, the prospect of returning to England, even though it meant leaving Luke behind, came as a welcome relief.

He wouldn't be away for long, Guy promised, as he boarded the EasyJet flight at Toulouse, but even within his own small world, much as he might have hoped, Guy could not control everything.

# 33

'The Frogs are revolting,' Pete told Sarah over breakfast. 'Paris is in flames, and even in Guy's quiet corner protesters are everywhere, blocking roads and intimidating everybody. Still, they've knackered the speed cameras, so some good may come of it.'

'What did he say when you saw him?'

Pete had met Guy in London a couple of days before, but had so far said nothing about it to Sarah. After being unexpectedly consigned to the couch for the night, he had not felt like telling her much of anything.

'He seems to think the protests will melt away out of boredom or inanition. Something I couldn't follow about dying from their internal contradictions. Evidently, it's a bogus alliance of left and right cobbled together on Facebook. He seems to have been reading some pretty whacky stuff.'

'Or smoking it.'

'I can tell he's worried.'

'Who isn't?'

'I mean about Luke. And all that money his mum left him. He wasn't expecting it.'

'He can always give it away.'

Pete wasn't sure if Sarah was trying to be funny. Humour had never been her strong suit.

'Knowing Guy, he might just do that.'

'He could start with us.' Pete wasn't sure about that 'us.' What us? 'After all, he owes his success to you.' Clearly not a joke then.

'Hardly. I'd have done the same for anyone with his talent.'

'I wonder.'

Pete wasn't sure about that 'I wonder.' Something to do with what she really thought of him and his friendship with Guy. But perhaps he was reading too much into it.

'I'd certainly have tried. Artists as good as Guy are as rare as unicorns, and need all the help they can get.'

'A few quid in our direction wouldn't go amiss.'

'Ask him.'

'I couldn't possibly.'

'You don't expect me to?'

'No.'

'Then why bring it up?'


Feeling guilty that he hadn't seen Jack on his previous visit, Pete had returned to Dorset for the weekend. In his mind he'd formulated a practical proposition which would allow Sarah and her son to return to London, and for Pete and Sarah to make one last go at their marriage. Both were lonely; neither was involved with anyone else; it seemed only sensible. Except that in the cold light of morning, sensible didn't seem remotely enough. Sensible had never been enough. So far he'd revealed nothing, and the longer he sat at the breakfast table, the more ridiculous his scheme appeared to him. There was too much history between them which could not be wished away. As for Jack, he now seemed almost a stranger. He had put on a growth spurt, and aged 11 was almost as tall as Pete; where once full of curiosity, virtually monosyllabic. Jack had been Pete's primary concern when planning their return to London, yet he wasn't sure the boy wanted to come back. For all that he may have fallen in with some pretty dodgy friends, Jack seemed content in his private world, hunched over his computer game, ears encased in head-phones, tapping away.

'We need to talk,' Pete told Sarah.

'Why?'

'I was thinking.'

'What about?'

Pete shook his head in frustration. He could see there was no point trying to talk to her.

'It doesn't matter.'

'OK. Be like that.'

But it was not OK. He could see that clearly now. In fact, he might as well admit that it was never going to be OK, not with Sarah anyway.

'Another time,' Pete said, picking up the newspaper, wishing he was somewhere else. Anywhere else.

## 34

'I warned you,' Bill said.

'I had to find out for myself.'

'You already knew. You just didn't want to accept it.'

'I can't believe how hard she's become. We were like strangers,' Pete said, shaking his head. 'It's so depressing. One minute you think you want to spend the rest of your life with someone, the next you wonder what you ever saw in them.'

Bill grinned.

'One minute the Prague Spring, the next the Russian Front!'

'It isn't funny.'

'Oh, I don't know.'

'It's painful.'

'You weren't seriously expecting her to welcome you with open arms? I mean legs.' Pete shrugged. 'She knew it wasn't her you really wanted. They usually can. You were just feeling lonely and wanted a cuddle. Nowt wrong in that.'

'That's not true. I really loved her.'

'Once maybe, not now. In your shoes I'd be feeling mightily relieved. Think what it would have been like to go through all the palaver of setting up home again, only to discover you had nothing in common.'

'I had to try. I had to make sure.'

'Now you know.'

## 35

Money had never meant much to Guy. He had grown up in a large comfortable house with live-in staff and a chauffeur to drive everyone around, and knew he was happiest without it. How else would he have found out what he truly wanted from life? A professional aquatint box to replace the gimcrack affair he'd knocked together; a wide-bed Rochat etching press; some long overdue repairs to the tower – those were what money could best provide. But to Alice, Guy's sudden, unexpected inheritance was a brilliant opportunity to transform their lives: they could sell the tower, with its basic plumbing and terrifying electrics. And they could finally leave France, where she had never felt welcome or comfortable.

'Leave?' Guy said, incredulous, over the phone. 'And go where?'

'Anywhere.'

'You know nothing's going to change.'

'So you always say.'

'I love my tower. I've never felt at home anywhere else.'

'Yes, well. This isn't only about you. You now have a family. Responsibilities.'

'And you have a typical foreigner's romantic idea of England. I went to one of those wonderful public schools you're so keen to send Luke to, and I would never put a son of mine through that.'

'That was half a century ago, before I was even born. These days they're like luxury hotels.'

'Another reason not to send him. The speed everything is changing, it's madness to plan too far ahead.'

'You have to do something. For Luke. For me too.'

'Stop worrying. It only makes Luke anxious. You'll be fine. I'll make sure of that. I promise.'

'You better.'

## 36

'What did I tell you? What did I always say? Just bread and circuses. Bread and bloody circuses,' Bill repeated, shaking his head.

Pete couldn't remember his friend so angry since missing an open goal in a football match at school.

'Leaving Europe was never going to be that easy. It's more like disentangling a long marriage.'

'What do you know about marriage? Brexit means Brexit, that's what the silly moo said, and I stupidly believed her. But it was all a sham. She was stringing us along and never had any intention of keeping her promise. But at least she's now gone. Useless woman was never up to the job. Did you see her on the box, blubbing about "the country I love"? About as sincere as the sodding Duke of Windsor telling Welsh miners something must be done when he knew he was about to jump ship with "the woman I love".' Bill shook his head. 'When Boris stepped into Downing Street, I felt like Rip van Winkle waking from a bloody coma. As if the last three mind-numbing years were a necessary prelude to something bright and beautiful. For the first time since the Falklands I felt proud to be British.' Bill glanced nervously at Pete. 'Yes, all right. I know I'm a naïve bloody fool. But sometimes one needs to be, just to get by.'

## 36

'Helen wants you to come for dinner,' Bill said, over lunch at the Fox & Grapes. 'There's someone she'd like you to meet.'

'Tell her thanks but no thanks. I'm better off on my own.'

'Bollocks. Everyone needs someone. Especially lonely old farts like you. Did you know that divorced or widowed men are said to be the most miserable fuckers of all?'

'Who are the happiest?'

'Women who've never lived with a man apparently.'

'I can believe that!'

'Helen read it in some silly glossy. One of those rags that always insist a pert bum is the first thing the female looks for in a man. By the way, she knows all about you and Sarah, if that's what's bothering you.' Pete frowned.

'Why did you have to tell her?'

'We have no secrets.'

'I'm sorry to hear that.'

'Frankly, it's a relief not having to hide things.'

Pete wondered what Bill had ever had to hide, and said: 'So she knows about your other family?'

'What other family?'

'In Uganda.'

Bill looked dumbfounded.

'Uganda?'

Pete nodded with mock gravity.

'The black one. Or should I say, of colour. The Chieftain's beautiful daughter. Surely you remember? She cost you a shedload in beads.'

'What the fuck are you talking about?'

Pete grinned.

'Just teasing. You looked so bloody serious.'

Bill shook his head.

'They're no joke, families. I worked all the hours God sent me to support just one, for all the thanks it ever got me.'

'Then why are you trying to hitch me up?'

'Not me Guv. I couldn't give a bugger what you do, but Helen wants everyone to be as happy as we are.'

After sitting for a while in companionable silence, Pete said: 'Still nothing from Ivan?'

Bill shrugged.

'It's his life, as he always insists.'

'I'd be properly pissed off.'

'Yes, well. You're not me.'

Bill could never conceal anything. He had one of those faces which manifested his every mood. 'Anyway, Helen says...' There was no need to finish the sentence. As in a long marriage, both knew exactly what Bill was going to say.

## 37

Pete's mobile rang.

'Hey Pete, it's Andrea.'

A voice from the past. An American voice that had always meant trouble but which Pete was surprised to find he was delighted to hear.

'Who?'

'Oh, I forgot. You never remember your old lovers.'

'Not the same Andrea who forgot to turn up at her own wedding?'

'I didn't forget. I took your advice.'

'What advice?'

'You told me not to marry Bill.'

'I'm sure I didn't.'

'You said it wouldn't work out and I believed you.'

'So you married someone else instead.'

'You know about that?'

'He was an old client of Bill's. All going well, I hope.'

'He died.'

Of what, Pete wondered, and said: 'Jesus, Andrea. How many's that?'

'Who's counting?'

'Not you, obviously.'

'You still with what's her name? The serious one. Miss No Sex.'

'You mean my wife?'

'Sorry. Mrs No Sex.'

'She's called Sarah.'

'Was that her name?'

'Yes. And no, we're no longer together.'

'Then I figure you're seeing someone else?'

'No one serious.'

'Well, all right!' the voice said, brightening.


'You mean you never told Bill?'

'About what?'

'About us.'

'Are you mad? He'd never have forgiven me and I'd never have forgiven myself.'

'It was great, wasn't it?'

'What I can remember of it.'

'You mean you weren't making that up? About not knowing where you were?'

Pete shook his head.

'I had a blackout.'

'I guess you were feeling guilty.'

How would you know? Pete wondered, and said: 'That's the only time it's happened to me.'

'That's because the sex was so great.'

'Was it?'

'Don't tease, Pete.'

'I never know when you're being serious.'

'I was serious about you. Always had been. Ever since joining your life-drawing class.'

'I never noticed.'

'Tell me about it!'

Pete agreed to meet Andrea for a cocktail, which had segued
into dinner and, unless he held his nerve, would no doubt lead
to their spending the night together. For all his many lovers,
Pete had never been adept at reading signs, and had often been
surprised when a woman went to bed with him. Andrea was
different. With her there was never any room for confusion or
doubt. She always said what she meant and asked for what she
wanted. She reminded Pete of the catalogue entry for a Sam-
urai sword which,despite having had three handles and four
blades, is described as 'original': hardly a part of Andrea hadn't
been replaced or upgraded, including her voice which now had
none of the high-pitched nasal twang Pete found unbearable
in American women. Only her hands betrayed her age.

'Been in touch with Bill?' Pete asked, over coffee.

Andrea shook her head.

'Why would I now he's with someone else?'

'Helen's delightful, and very good for him,' Pete said. 'Much
more suitable, I have to say.'

'You mean I wasn't?'

'Not in the least. Don't get me wrong. He was crazy about
you. Even now he won't hear a word against you.'

'Honestly Pete, how could I marry him? He was still in love with his dead wife, for Chrissakes.'

'You'd have soon got bored. He wouldn't have known what to do with you.'

'Unlike you, you mean?'

'I wasn't available. You already knew that.'

'You're never available. That's what makes you so attractive.'


'What's my name?' asked Andrea, snuggling closer to Pete.

'Which one? You've had so many.'

'OK. Where are we?'

'Your flat.'

'Address?'

'How should I know? Somewhere in Chelsea. Why?'

'Just checking,' Andrea said, nuzzling the back of his neck.


'I'm thinking of moving over here full-time. The way the States is going...'

'Trump?'

'Not just him. The whole deal. I don't feel safe anymore.'

'You think it's better here?'

'Feels that way,' she said, nimble fingers running up Pete's thigh.


'I've all this dough and no kids,' Andrea said, over breakfast, 'So I may as well spend it having a good time.'

'Why not do something useful with it?'

'Oh yeah? Like what?'

'I've no idea. Support poor students. Endow a scholarship. Something meaningful.'

'You mean like struggling artists?'

'Possibly.'

From the way she was smiling, Pete knew what she was thinking, and shook his head. 'Someone far more deserving than me.'

'Jesus Pete, why do you always put yourself down?'

'Do I? I've never noticed. To quote that great philosopher Dirty Harry, a man has to know his limitations.'

'That's crap. You just never tried.'

'You're quite wrong. Unlike most people, I know my precise limitations. Why do you think I live alone?'

'You never met the right woman. Until now.'

## 38

Bill asked Pete to help him out. 'Helen keeps insisting she has the perfect person for you. I tell her you're not interested, but she won't take no for an answer.'

'Say I've met someone. That should do it.'

'I won't lie to her.'

'What if it's true?'

'Is it?'

'Could be...'

'Love is like golf,' Bill said, as they sat in the 19th hole, taking shelter from the pouring rain. 'It all comes down to timing. I used never to mind about the weather, but recently I've turned into a real wuss. Not my Helen. Even now she's out there somewhere,' he said, peering through the steamed-up picture window: 'Bang, bang, bang, straight down the middle every time, like an effing metronome. I don't know how she does it.'

'She must get very bored.'

'Never seems to.'

'Doesn't she miss digging around in all that heather looking for her ball? It's a big part of the game.'

'Never has to.'

'How can you stand it?'

'It isn't easy,' Bill said, grinning.


'All right. Who is she, and when do we get to meet her?' Bill asked, returning from the bar with more drinks.

'Who says it's a her?' Bill patted Pete on the knee.

'So you've finally come out? No surprise there, then.'

Pete smiled.

'Just easing the door open.'

'Very funny. You're the least queer person I know.'

'Sometimes I wish I were. It would make life so much easier.'

'A fuck of a lot more complicated, if you ask me.'

'Let's just say there may be someone. I can't say more.'

Bill tapped the side of his nose.

'Married?'

Pete nodded.

'Frequently.'

'So she knows what she's doing?'

'Or not!'

'Doesn't seem to have affected your game. That's usually the first sign.'

'Of what?'

'Mind not fully on the job.'

Pete shrugged.

'I know how to compartmentalise.'

'I wish I did. With me, everything just runs into every-thing else.'

'When did you last have your prostate checked?' Pete asked.

'Don't joke. It isn't funny at our age.'

'I used to know by the wind when my flies were open,' Pete said. 'Now I can no longer tell.'

'No doubt your new friend will help you out.'

'I certainly hope so!'


### 39


Pete was relieved to be teaching again. Before turning 60, he'd often wondered what retirement would bring, imagining his days filled with all the things he'd never had time for and hoped to do before he died. But it hadn't turned out like that. His one concrete project, an illustrated guide to East Anglian churches, combining his interest in local history with his skills as a draughtsman, had been abandoned when he and Sarah parted, and he'd been forced to let go of the rented Suffolk cottage where they'd spent most weekends.

'You never seem to have a free moment. You're always on the go,' Pete had told Bill three years earlier, after he'd been unexpectedly given the push by the art school. 'I really admire that. All I do is sit on my arse all day, waiting for something to happen and wondering where the years have gone.'

'Too much thinking. That's why I keep busy. Something will turn up. Just don't push it.'

Pete smiled at this vestige of New Age Bill. But his words failed to resonate with Pete, who was used to knowing where he needed to be at any given time of day, and for whom this sudden, unplanned absence of structure was a burden rather than an opportunity – unlike his friend and former pupil Guy, who was always working yet also seemed to lead a rich, full family life in rural France. Aimless and dissatisfied, unemployed and alone, Pete had spent far too much of his retirement in the pub, so the job had come as a lifeline.

'It's my own fault,' he said. 'I should have planned more carefully. But I was always busy and there still seemed so much time. Now we're living it, I feel like an alien. I don't understand a bloody word this new generation says to me. They could be speaking a foreign language.'

'They are.'

'Where the hell do they get all their potty ideas?'

'From the Yanks, no doubt.' Bill shook his head. 'Unlike you, I'd no choice. With a wife and three young kids and a business to run, I had to plan ahead. When Carol suddenly chucked in her City job to become a bloody shrink, muggins here had to pick up the slack. Either that or downsize and take the kids out of private school, which I was never going to do. Still, I sometimes wonder if it wasn't a mistake investing so much in them. They don't seem to have turned out any different to other young people, Ivan especially.'

'Don't underestimate him. I know the two of you aren't getting on, but there's something special about my Godson. One day he'll do something to make you very proud. I know it.'

88

'He'd bloody better. The ungrateful little sod. When I think how much he's cost me...'

40

'Bill keeps asking, so I'll have to say something,' Pete told Andrea, as they lay in bed one sunny Saturday morning. 'It's only fair.'

'To who?'

'Whom.'

'God, you can be a pedantic bastard,' she said digging her nails into his back. 'Anyway, what's the goddam hurry? It's not as if we're getting married.'

'Suppose he hears from someone else?'

'Who cares?'

'I do.'

'How much were you planning to say?'

'I hadn't thought. I don't want to upset him.'

'Nothing about that first time?'

'Certainly not.'

'Forget it ever happened.'

'You mean the way I did at the time!'

Andrea shook her head. Why were men so dumb when it came to emotion? And why did they never know when to keep their mouths shut? She had so hoped Pete would prove different. She always hoped the next man would be different.

'Tell him it happened for the first time the other day, when I was passing through London. That it came as a complete surprise.'

'It did.'

'For you, maybe.'

'Yes, OK,' he said, embracing her.

'Trust me,' she said, biting his forearm. 'I've been here before. I know what I'm talking about.'


## 41

'I didn't want to speak prematurely,' Pete told Bill. 'I wasn't sure you'd understand.'

'What's there to understand? When two people...'

'That's easy to say, but is that what you feel?'

'It's certainly unexpected.'

'Surprised?'

'She isn't the first person who came to mind.'

'And you really don't mind?'

Bill shrugged.

'Not much effing point if I do, is there?'

'To be honest, I was gobsmacked. Still am. But as you always say, timing is everything. Like you and Helen,' Pete added.

'Indeed. I only wish I'd met her sooner.'

'Be thankful you met her at all.'

'Believe me, I am. I say a little prayer every day.'

'Me too.'


## 42

Guy was back in London, dealing with some aspect of his mother's estate, and popped into the art school to see Pete.

When the lunch bell rang, they walked around the corner to the pub.

'You don't want to come back here to live, do you?' Pete asked.

Guy shook his head.

'I may have no choice.'

'Brexit?'

'Alice.'

Guy stared into his glass of fizzy water. It was twenty years since he'd last drunk alcohol, and until recently he had never missed it. Now he wondered what, if anything, he might still be trying to prove, and if there was any point holding back. 'I keep being told it isn't just about me. She doesn't like being stuck in the middle of nowhere and detests the French. And Luke needs to be around children his own age, intelligent children, not the feral offspring of local peasants. So maybe she has a point. I don't know.'

'It's time you had another show. What are you working on?'

'I can't talk about it.'

'Not even to me?'

As his friend and former teacher, Pete had always been the one person with whom Guy felt free to discuss his work.

'Perhaps. I don't know. If I could put it into words...'

'You'd never do it.'

Guy nodded.

'Pretty much.'

For a while they sat eating their sandwiches in silence. Then Guy leaned over the back of his chair and took out a battered ipad from his shoulder bag. 'Here,' he said, handing it to Pete. 'You asked for it. Don't pull your punches. I need to know.'

'You flatter me.'

Guy shrugged.

'Usually it's the other way around.'

'I won't say anything I don't mean. You know that.'

'I wouldn't have asked otherwise.' Guy stood up and began to walk away. 'I need to stretch my legs.'

'See you then.'

'No dissimulation. Only the unvarnished truth.'

'Yes, all right. Bugger off.'


'You don't like them, do you? I can tell,' Guy said, uncharacteristically nervous, when he finally returned from his walk. Pete had been wondering where he'd got to as he needed to get back to the art school.

'Whether I do or not is beside the point.'

'Not to me.'

'Look, I have to go. Can we talk later?'

Pete felt distracted. He needed time to assess the impact of Guy's work and to consider a proper response. To be asked one's opinion by a serious artist is a responsibility as much as a privilege, and never to be undertaken lightly.

'Can't you tell me now?'

'I don't want to rush this. It isn't fair on you. Or me, for that matter.'

Pete couldn't remember Guy ever caring what anyone else thought, least of all about his work. In spite of himself, the words now came tumbling out.

'All right, how's this? Visceral. Harrowing. Naked. Exposed. Will that do?'

'It's a start.'

Pete knew he sounded angry, when what he really felt was wounded. Guy's new work was like a punch in the stomach, dragging Pete into some sinister dark place from which he had felt desperate to escape, from which even now he had barely recovered.

'You did ask.'

'I know. I just wasn't expecting...'

Pete touched Guy's arm.

'For me to be so affected?'

'Maybe. You know how hard it is sometimes,' Guy said. 'How buttoned up we English are.' And then, when Pete still said nothing: 'I blame my mother.'

Pete chuckled, although he suspected Guy wasn't joking, and said: 'Don't we all?'

'Remember how I used to spend all my time drawing people in crowded places, where everyone was too busy to pay me any attention? I felt wonderfully anonymous. I've hundreds of old sketchbooks which I must have intended as a source for painting. But the moment I discovered Morandi I packed all that in. It suddenly seemed completely irrelevant.'

'Those marvellous empty landscapes, entirely devoid of people.'

Guy nodded.

'The silence must have been a great relief.'

'For a while I've been feeling I'd lost something. I was no longer me. And I needed to find my way back. Mother's death was the catalyst. My biggest fear is that it may already be too late.'

'You mean you did all these in the last few weeks?'

'The last few days, actually,' Guy said, smiling shyly. 'You know me.'

Pete shook his head in disbelief.

'That's incredible.'

'It's been bubbling away for a long time.'

'Timing is all.'

Guy smiled.

'What I'd really like now is a drink.'

'Think you should?'

'I know I shouldn't.'

'Then don't. I've never asked why you gave up.'

'It's like Tolstoy on marriage. All alcoholics are miserable in much the same way. Some people alcohol makes benign...'

'Bill's like that. I'm not sure I don't prefer him pissed.'

'He's not an alki. He just drinks too much. With me it was the opposite. Twenty-odd years ago I woke up after an eight-hour blackout and decided enough was enough.'

'Seems a pretty good reason. Miss it?'

Guy shook his head.

'Not till now.'

'When my mother died I drank like a fish,' Pete said. 'Didn't do any good. I mean, it didn't bring me any closer to my real feelings. It just made me wonder if I had any.'

'It's a bit late in the day to worry about things like that.'

'It's never too late. You have a family, responsibilities. And you have your amazing work. I've only a bunch of lazy, know-nothing students who disagree with everything I say.'

'And Andrea. Don't forget her.'

Pete smiled.

'Yes, and Andrea.'

'If anyone can put them straight, you can.'

'I'm not sure I've the energy. Or the inclination. They have to learn from their own mistakes. As we all did. Still do.'

'Or not.'

'You have.'

'Maybe. I don't know. If I have, a lot of it's thanks to you.'

'Not really.'

'Stop knocking yourself,' Guy said. 'Without you, I'd never have shown my stuff to anyone.'

'You'd have found a way. You're far too good. Anyone else would have done the same.'

'Don't you believe it.'

'I'm afraid I do.'

'It's not just me. Whether you know it or not, you've made a hell of a difference to a lot of peoples' lives, and that's more than most of us can ever claim.'

Pete reddened with embarrassment.

'Thanks,' he said, and he meant it.

## 43

'My real problem with Remainers,' Bill repeated, 'is that even though none of their dire prognostications have been remotely fulfilled, they still insist that's solely because we haven't yet left. Instead of feeling relieved, their only concern is with being proved right. Typical seaside landlady mentality.'

'I don't feel that way,' Pete said.

'You were never that bothered.'

'I'm not ideological, if that's what you mean. I favoured staying because it seemed a hell of a lot to go through for a pretty uncertain future. Now, like most people, I just want it over.'

'Remainers behave as if the arguments for Europe are self-evident, so even after four years no one has bothered to make the case for staying in. You know why?'

Pete shook his head. Brexit was one of Bill's *bêtes noire*, and Pete knew it didn't matter what he said. 'Because there isn't one. The only way the EU can survive is through greater integration, and we were never going to sign up to that. So better to get out now. Whenever they have a crisis they pretend nothing's wrong, but in reality it's every man for himself, as it always has been, and the little guy gets thrown to the wolves by the greedy Hun or the perfidious Frog. As de Gaulle rightly said, "we shall stun you with our ingratitude." Fancy another?' Bill added, picking up his empty glass.

'Better not. I have to collect Andrea's car from the garage.'

'Got you by the short and curlies, hasn't she? I should have warned you.'

Pete shook his head.

'Just helping her out.'

'Having a facial, is she? Or is it her Pilates class? Oh sorry, I forgot. If it's Wednesday, it must be emotional cord cutting. Or do I mean aromatherapy? Must be hard keeping up with all that shit.'

For some time Pete had been wondering where Bill put his anger, and it was at last coming out.

'You used to like all that.'

'Not really.'

Pete had come to admire the vigilance with which Andrea regarded her body, even if he couldn't always see the point in fighting time so relentlessly. He liked her just the way she was, even if, as she was the first to admit, it wasn't all original.

'How does it feel to be a kept man?'

'I wouldn't know.'

'She's very high maintenance. But I expect you know that.'

'I pay my way. It may not be much, but it's all I can afford.'

Bill's remark had touched a raw nerve. Sarah had on occasion said much the same thing, accusing Pete of meanness when, living on his meagre salary, he had no choice; and even if, unlike Sarah, Andrea didn't mind, that didn't make Pete any more comfortable with it. He had never been in debt and didn't like to feel beholden, and every gift from Andrea, every treat, large or small paid for by her, put Pete, in his own eyes at least, at a disadvantage, and Bill knew it.

'Why does it bother you?' Pete asked.

'It doesn't.'

'I thought you didn't mind.'

'I don't.'

'You know you're much happier with Helen.'

'Infinitely.'

'Then why are you so cross?'

For a few moments Bill looked uncharacteristically thoughtful.

'Maybe I can't stand you always looking like the cat's that's got all the effing cream.'

'You mean the way you do?'

Bill nodded.

'Maybe.'

'Perhaps I will have another, after all,' Pete said.

'Buy it yourself. And while you're at it,' Bill added, shoving his empty glass at Pete, 'I'll have one too. Make it a large one.'

'Any idea of her age? I mean her real age.' Bill asked.

'Who, Andrea? Not exactly, but I can probably guess.'

'Go on.'

Reluctantly, Pete mentioned a number, at which Bill snorted and grinned triumphantly.

'And the rest. I once saw her passport.'

Pete shrugged.

'Good for her is all I can say. More power to her elbow.'

'Don't you mind?'

'Not in the least. You're not bothered about Helen.'

'What about Helen?'

'Her being much older than you.'

'Who says she is?'

'Oh, honestly Bill. Who gives a toss anyway?'

'I thought you might, given your predilection for...'

'For what?'

'Young flesh.'

'That's all in the past. Anyway, they're no longer interested in me. I can't understand a word they say.'

'That never stopped you.'

'I wasn't in it for the conversation. The young today are entirely different, in case you haven't noticed.'

'They've got much bigger tits. I've noticed that!'

'Too much dairy' Pete said. 'You can't say anything remotely suggestive in case they take it the wrong way. And to be honest I'm no longer interested in anyone else.'

'I don't believe you. Leopards and spots.'

'Believe what you like. I was pretty faithful to Sarah.'

'Whatever that means! In 30 years of marriage I never looked at another woman.'

'Oh, really? What about all those sporting tours?'

'That was different. What goes on tour, stays on tour.'

'How very convenient!'

'Carol never knew, which is what matters.'

'How do you know she didn't?'

'I just do,' Bill said. 'Why, what did you tell her?'

'Nothing. What do you take me for? But what about her? You don't seriously imagine you were her one and only?'

'Certainly.'

'And if you found out you weren't?'

'I'd never forgive her.'

'Even though she's been dead for years and you're now in love with someone else?'

'Yes.'

Pete patted Bill's arm.

'Don't worry. I'm sure she wasn't.'

'I bloody well hope not.'

## 44

'I always wondered what being old felt like. Now I know,' Pete told Andrea over breakfast.

'You look great.' She slid her hand under his dressing gown. 'Feel great, too.'

'My hips ache, my knees ache. My hands are stiff in the mornings.'

'Not just your hands!'

'I think about death the whole time.'

'Not all of it, I hope.'

He looked at her and smiled. Feeling conciliatory, he added: 'I expect it's the time of year. These short days before Christmas always depress me.'

The clocks had just gone back, and that evening there was a Halloween party in the building, full of screaming kids in scary costumes, which was Pete's idea of hell. For days he'd been wondering how he might get out of it. Not for the first time, he said:

'Do I really have to come?'

'No.'

'But you hope I will.'

'Not if you don't want to.'

'Do you really mean that?'

'No.'

'All right, I'll come. But only if I don't have to dress up.'


In a few days' time Andrea was leaving for the USA to spend Thanksgiving with her family. Despite numerous marriages she had no children of her own, but any number of nephews and nieces, whose wide ingenuous faces and perfect teeth grinned out from photographs all over her flat. Pete couldn't remember seeing them on his first visit five years before, but he still recalled little of that momentous afternoon, even if, to mollify Andrea, he now sometimes pretended he did.

'Ten days, max. You're welcome to come along. I know they'd just love to meet you.'

'Another time.'

Pete wondered how often in her life she had held similar conversations with other men. In his mind's eye he saw Andrea's family eyeing each other anxiously as they wondered who their zany aunt would turn up with that year.

'When did you last see them? I mean on your own.'

'It's been a while.'

'Then they'd probably like to have you to themselves.'

'I guess so,' she said flatly, sounding as depressed as Pete.

One Friday afternoon six months earlier, Pete had arrived at Andrea's flat carrying an overnight bag. Both had assumed he was only coming for the weekend, but he had returned after school on the Monday and every evening for the following fortnight, until she at last suggested he move in. As if in the throes of some terminal illness, the future was never spoken of, nor any terms agreed between them. She would let him pay for cinema tickets and take-aways, and even the occasional fry-up in a favourite café which she claimed to enjoy even when he could see she didn't; and some evenings, he would return with a bottle of wine or a bunch of flowers. But if they went anywhere expensive, where Pete suspected she felt more comfortable, it was understood that she would pick up the bill.

At first, he had been as reluctant to investigate her colourful past as she was to volunteer information. He knew there'd been a number of husbands but not how many or what had befallen them. For each of them, their affair represented a new beginning, and while pretending to feel no jealousy, each was cautious about revealing too much. In love herself, Andrea couldn't imagine other women not being in love with

Pete, whereas he regarded her marriages as mere practice sessions during which she had honed her swing in preparation for the real match ahead.

Pete felt ashamed of himself for not having noticed her interest in him all those years before, for behind her directness lay a tenderness he had always hoped to find in Sarah but never had. That Andrea might also be conniving and manipulative, the very words Pete had once used to describe her to Bill, now seemed well wide of the mark. A step to the left, a step to the right, and the whole picture changes, as Pete liked to remind his students; as he had once tried to convince Andrea, whose clumsy efforts at producing a pictorial likeness had made Pete wince. Now, for perhaps the first time, he accepted that others might just see things differently.

'You will be back for Christmas? I'd hate to be on my own, and can't face going to Bill and Helen, though I know they'd have me.'

'Sure thing. Unless maybe you want to meet up somewhere warm. Chill out in the sunshine, Cancun or Saint Barts?'

'I can't afford it.'

'My treat,' Andrea insisted, but Pete shook his head.

'I mean it.'

'So do I.'

She thought for a moment. Then, smiling, said: 'OK. How's about we compromise. You find somewhere cosy in the country with big open fires and nice romantic walks, and I'll pick up the tab.' Pete returned her smile.

'OK. Done.'

## 45

For much of his long marriage, Bill's social life had followed a prescribed routine which skilfully combined pleasure with business. Since Carol's death and the sale of his advertising agency, he had cut right back and found to his surprise that he missed almost none of it. He no longer had demanding clients to entertain, and sport was much better watched on TV; large social gatherings, where once he'd relished being the centre of attention, were now, with his poor hearing, more a chore than pleasure. But in no case did he feel the change was in him. Invariably, it was the wider world which was at fault.

Carol had known how to tease him. Without her, he was in danger of becoming an opinionated old fart; something Helen, for all that she adored him, was only too aware of. Despite his bluster, she found him at times surprisingly lacking in self-confidence, and the last thing she wanted was to undermine him, even if that meant having to listen to the same old stories far more often than she would have liked. Though Bill was easy to poke fun at, few people were ever nasty about him, and Helen and Pete could often be found on the sofa in Wimbledon, sharing funny stories about Bill who, unable to hear what they were saying, went on happily fabricating his ever more lethal cocktails.

'What's this one called,' Pete asked, spluttering as the initial taste slammed into the back of his throat. Bill tapped his nose.

'Something I found in the *Savoy Cocktail Book*, but I've added a few refinements of my own. I couldn't get blue curaçao, so I've made do with Cointreau.' Bill grinned mischievously. 'Pretty sporting, what?'

'It's got one hell of a kick.'

Bill handed Helen a tall coloured glass, topped with a maraschino cherry and paper umbrella.

'I'll think I'll stick to sherry,' Helen said.

'Very wise, my Angel.'

'Are we celebrating something?' Pete asked, aware of a sudden change of atmosphere. Bill and Helen exchanged glances. Then Helen took charge.

'How did you guess? Bill's insisted on making an honest woman of me. I told him I didn't care one way or the other, but he wasn't having any of it. You know how traditional he is.'

She smiled tenderly, then took Bill's hand, an action which pleased Pete but left him feeling oddly excluded. He realised just how much he was missing Andrea, who had twice postponed her return from the USA. Knocking back the remains of his cocktail, Pete handed his empty glass back to Bill for a refill.

'So you're proposing to tie the knot?' Pete asked, looking from one to the other.

'All done and dusted, old boy,' Bill said. 'Sorry we didn't let you in on it. As a matter of fact, we haven't told anyone.'

'Not even the kids?'

Bill shook his head.

'But they do know?'

'No. Not yet. But...'

'Just as soon as we're back from our world cruise,' Helen chipped in, finishing Bill's sentence for him, as she did more and more these days.

'World cruise, eh? Isn't that rather pushing the boat out? I mean, being all at sea when you barely know each other?'

'We already know each other quite well enough, thanks very much,' Bill said, finding nothing funny in Pete's remark, while Helen raised her sherry glass and glowed contentedly.

## 46

Some people signpost their lives according to their jobs, their holidays, even their marriages: that was when I was doing this or that, when I went here or there, or was living with so and so. For Bill, life was best measured by his enthusiasms: a game, like cricket, rugby, or golf; an author or composer he had devoured wholesale (Evelyn Waugh, George Gershwin); a hobby, like wine or medal collecting which for a time had dominated his life.

During his mystic phase, as Pete still referred to that curious period following Bill's 60th birthday, when in a matter of months he had shed five stone and acquired a whole new portfolio of far-fetched beliefs, it was anything to do with saving the planet. The unexpected return of Carol's cancer had brought him back to earth with a bang. Though never again the fat, jolly bon vivant he had been in his heyday, he no longer regarded self-indulgence as a crime or pleasure something to be ashamed of. Then Helen came into his life, and any remaining vestiges of self-control were abandoned in a frantic crusade to turn back the years before it was too late.

'Where's he gone?' Pete asked Helen. Bill had been out of the room for twenty minutes and Pete was getting worried. 'Is he OK?'

Helen nodded.

'I don't suppose he'd tell me if there was something wrong.'

'Probably not.'

'If you really want to know, he's cooking.'

'Crikey. I hope you've got a good doctor.'

'I can't keep him out of the kitchen, which suits me to a tee, as I'm completely hopeless.'

'You can't be good at everything.'

'Hopeless!' she repeated, smiling at Pete.

'Any particular cuisine?' Pete asked.

'Curries. The hotter the better.'

Pete pulled a face.

'I can't eat that stuff.'

'Me neither. He's promised us something mild tonight.'

'Still doing his photography?' With Bill, it was usually one hobby at a time, to the exclusion of everything else.

'I'm afraid so.'

'You don't approve?'

She shrugged.

'It's more the subject matter.'

'No more crop circles then?'

'If only!'

'Don't tell me. Naked women?'

'How did you know?'

'I was joking. But I always suspected that somewhere in Bill a pornographer was lurking in the shadows.'

'It isn't funny. The other day he asked me to pose. In the buff, of all things. Well, how could I, a woman my age? Just look at me.'

Pete smiled.

'I completely disagree. To him you're beautiful, which is all that matters. Stanley Spencer was the same. To him, getting your kit off was the most natural thing in the world, even if he did abandon his loving wife for a lesbian who wouldn't go to bed with him. Ever seen his Leg of Mutton nude? Wonderful picture.' She shook her head. 'So watch out in case he ever asks you to pose with a bowl of Vindaloo.'

Helen smiled back.

'He's turned Ivan's bedroom into a dark room. I told him I didn't think it was a good idea, but he wouldn't listen. I know Ivan doesn't approve of me. I still haven't met him, though Millie's been lovely from the start. But this is still Ivan's home, and he needs to know that.'

'They both do.'

'Perhaps, while we're away...'

'Yes, of course. To be honest, I'm surprised Ivan hasn't been in touch. He knows he can say whatever he likes to me.'

'He doesn't know about the bedroom. They haven't spoken in months.'

'I'll have a word.'

'You are a dear.'

A beaming, apron-clad Bill appeared in the doorway, tapping wooden spoons together.

'Grub's up,' he announced, bowing towards Helen. 'Come along my queen. Chop chop!'

## 47

'They were holding hands in the fucking street. At their age.'
Ivan said. 'It's disgusting.'

'I find it rather touching,' Pete said. 'It reveals yet another
facet of your old man's complex personality.'

'What personality?'

'Wait and see how you feel at seventy.'

'I never shall. None of us will. The planet's fucked and it's
all his fault.'

'Bill alone?' Pete said, restraining a smile he knew would
only further rile Ivan.

'All of you then.'

'I thought you hadn't met Helen.'

'Millie filled me in on the sordid details. if you really want
to know, I find it grotesque.'

'A little old-fashioned romance never did anyone any harm,'
Pete said. 'Especially at our advanced age.'

'Absolutely grotesque,' Ivan repeated, shaking his head.

# PART TWO

A cloud no bigger than a man's hand, a pebble dropped into a pond, sending ripples around the globe...


1


As the *Queen Mary* sailed from Southampton, en route to Lisbon, Bill and Helen settled into their luxurious penthouse apartment.

'Let's have a glass of bubbly and wave at the arse end of England,' Bill said. 'No need to unpack. There's a chap who does it all for us.'

'I'd rather do it myself. I don't like the thought of a stranger going through my things.' She smiled shyly. 'Won't be long.'

'Missing you already,' Bill said, glancing over his shoulder as he stepped out onto their private terrace and filled his lungs with bracing sea air.

Though his parents had left a note, apparently co-authored, Bill had never accepted the Coroner's verdict of double suicide, and remained convinced that his father, suffering from an undisclosed illness, had somehow talked his wife into joining him on his journey into the unknown. Unlike their overweight son, they had always kept fit, taking regular cruises to escape the British winter, from where the occasional deadpan missive would arrive in Wimbledon: cheap coloured postcards, usually of ruins, listing everything they had seen and done, but never bothering to ask after Bill or his family. An unnamed couple sometimes travelled with them, whom Bill had christened the Wilberforces, and whose corporeal existence, before the funeral, Bill had always doubted, for his parents had neither friends nor polite conversation. Their whole lives had been spent, as much as is humanly possible in a cramped country like England, by themselves and for themselves.

Bill had always dreaded those postcards. They stank of complacency and self-satisfaction and reinforced the view he had always held that, to use a military phrase he was particularly fond of, he was surplus to requirements. As a consequence, Bill had determined from the start to be a very different kind of parent, rejoicing in the smallest accomplishments of his offspring, and subsequently had little to feel ashamed of. Even Ivan, furious at the obscene sums he believed his father to be frittering away on frivolous entertainment, could not deny that.

'Can we afford this?' Helen asked, as they stood side by side at the rail, gazing into the setting sun. 'It must have cost a fortune.'

Bill shrugged.

'Anything for you, my darling.'

The idea of splashing out on a top-of-the-range world cruise would not normally have occurred to Bill, who preferred dry land, but meeting Helen had changed everything. Conscious because of her age – she was five years older than him – that they might not have that long together, he had stopped worrying about the future and concentrated all his energies on making every day as pleasurable as possible. He was always giving her presents, and if at times Helen didn't know how to respond, she came to accept that such generosity was as much for his sake as hers.

'Shall we go down?' she asked, suddenly feeling the chill.

'Pop inside and get warm. I'll join you in a minute,' Bill said, thinking unexpectedly of Carol as he gazed into the dark, choppy waters.


'Fancy a flutter?' Bill suggested, taking Helen's arm as they left the dining room.

'Why not? First night out and all that.'

Bill gleefully rubbed his hands together.

'Blackjack? Roulette? Whatever eez Madame's pleasure?'

'Roulette, please. Just the thought of it makes me shiver. Remember those wonderful old black and white films, full of glamorous blondes and smouldering continentals, with a piano tinkling away in the background and masses of cigar smoke. And all those lovely clothes.'

'The name's Bond. James Bond,' Bill said, imitating Sean Connery's Scottish brogue.

'Charles Boyer. Paul Henreid. Remember him lighting two cigarettes at once on a ship just like ours? He transformed Bette Davis overnight from a frumpy spinster into the epitome of glamour, and when she went home her awful mother didn't recognise her.'

'You were never frumpy. I've seen those old golfing photos. I'd have killed for a swing like yours.'

'Jim said I had swimmer's shoulders.'

'What was his bloody handicap?'

'11 at his best. He was desperate to play off single figures but never quite made it. It made him so cross.'

'Good. What made him such a bloody expert on feminine beauty?'

'He wasn't that interested.'

'Too busy worrying about his handicap, I expect.'

'Unlike you, my darling.'

'I don't want to know. I don't like to think of you with anyone else.'

'You mustn't worry about the past. We all have them. Unavoidable at our age.'

'Don't remind me.'

'There's nowhere else in the world I'd rather be,' Helen hummed.

'That's a song, isn't it?' Bill said, momentarily embarrassed. 'And no one else I'd rather be with.'

Bill grinned as he patted her arm, just like the happy little boy he'd never been.


## 2


Andrea flew into London just before Christmas, and immediately Pete knew something was wrong. Even by her standards she was trying too hard, perhaps for his sake as much as hers. He wanted to ask, but didn't know how, and wondered if the change was in him rather than Andrea. He had greatly missed her, but when she had kept postponing her return, he had shut down, and put on what Sarah referred to as his 'Easter Island' face. It was his way of coping with disappointment, and from which, to his frustration, he found he could never readily switch himself back on.

'What's going on Pete?' she asked over breakfast on her second day back. Since waking, he had hardly said a word to her, and they were off to the country that afternoon to spend the Christmas holiday together.

'Nothing. Still me.'

'All of you?'

'I presume so.'

'What the fuck does that mean?'

'It means that as far as I know, this is the real me. All there is of it, anyway.'

'Let's start again,' Andrea said. Pete nodded.

'You go first.'

'Why me?'

'Someone has to.'

He could see she was trying to hold things together and wasn't making much of a job of it.

'What's happened?' he asked. She shook her head.

'Nothing.'

'You seem different.'

'Do I?'

There was something uncharacteristically defiant about Andrea which discouraged further enquiry. It was no more than a hunch and Pete knew he might be wrong, and he didn't want to sour the mood any further. For all that he hated Christmas, the last thing he wanted was a fight with her, especially over something which might be of no importance. Unlike Sarah, she always seemed to know how to get the best out of him, even when the old impulses hung around, encouraging retreat.

'It's me,' he said. 'I missed you and was sad when you kept delaying your return. I felt you didn't care.'

'I had stuff to do. Stuff I couldn't put off any longer.'

He raised his eyebrows, hoping to encourage her to open up.

'One of your ex's? You know you can tell me,' Pete insisted.

'Can I?'

'I promise I won't mind.'

She brewed a fresh pot of coffee, then sat down at the kitchen table and lit a cigarette.

'I thought you'd given up'

'Me too.'

For a while they sat in silence, the tapping of her coffee spoon filling the space between them. Pete wanted to get up but felt glued to his chair. They were only a table's width apart but the gap seemed unbridgeable. Then, all of a sudden, Andrea began talking, and it was twenty minutes before Pete could get a word in.

'Jesus, where did all that come from?'

'Beats me,' she said, shaking her head.

'It must come from somewhere.'

'I guess so.'

'I've never heard you speak like that before.'

'I never did. You're the first person I ever told any of that stuff.'

'I'm flattered,' he said covering her hand. 'It shows you trust me.'

'Do you mind?'

Pete thought for a moment. It wasn't a question he'd ever been asked, nor one he'd ever asked himself.

'Far from it. It makes me very happy.'

'Really?' she asked, sounding unconvinced. Pete squeezed her hand.

'It makes me feel needed.'

'You sure as hell are,' she said, forcing a smile as she stubbed out her half-smoked cigarette.


3


'Like it?' Pete asked, pushing open the creaky front door. The thatched cottage felt damp and musty.

'It's kinda... rustic.'

'I thought that's what you wanted. A touch of ye olde England.'

'Feels like no one's been here in a hundred years.'

'They probably haven't. I found it in a magazine called *The Lady*.'

'Sounds like porn for cross dressers! You're not aiming to change sides, are you, Pete?'

'It's a highly respectable journal. Helen recommended it. Look,' he said, poking his head round a corner, 'It's even got a fridge. Well, sort of.'

He turned on the gas cooker. 'These all seem to work, so we won't starve.'

Moments later he heard footsteps overhead, then the sound of bed springs and floorboards. 'How is it?' he called out.

'Freezing. Sags in the middle.'

'Like me!'

There was the noise of moaning pipes and a boiler belching.

'It's perfect,' Andrea said, clattering down the old wooden staircase in six-inch heels, flashing Pete a bright, brittle smile.

'Let's go to the pub,' Pete said, taking her hand.

4

In no time, Bill and Helen settled into a regular shipboard routine: morning coffee out of their own silver pot, followed by a full breakfast in the main restaurant, after which they would promenade arm in arm around the deck, before returning to their suite, where Helen would sun herself on their private terrace under a wide-brimmed hat and Bill read books of Imperial history. After a light lunch, Helen played bridge while Bill, determined to better Jim's handicap, smacked golf balls into a net. Cocktails on the terrace at sunset to the squawking of seagulls, was followed by a slap-up dinner, for which Bill insisted they wear evening dress. Within a week he was struggling to fasten his cummerbund.

'Bloody rabble,' Bill said, eyeing the other guests, none of whom had bothered to change. 'Why come at all when half the fun is taking a bit of trouble?' Bill refilled his wineglass to the brim.

'Not too much, darling. It puts you in a bad mood.'

'Peasants,' Bill said, shaking his head.

'Shall we dance?'

'I'm not in the mood. Oh well, yes, all right.'

At Helen's suggestion, they had recently taken ballroom dancing classes, where Bill, to his astonishment, had been assured that he had very good footwork. He only wished a coach had said the same of any of the sports he'd struggled with all his life. To a foxtrot played especially for them, Bill and Helen moved lightly across the dance floor, watched by other guests. When they sat down there was a burst of spontaneous applause, and even a wolf whistle or two.

'Are they taking the piss?'

'I'm sure not.'

'Because if they are...'

'How about a romantic movie. Holding hands in the dark. Popcorn?'

'There's nothing I want to see.'

'A moonlit stroll around the deck?' she said, trying to humour him.

'Yes, OK,' Bill said, his mood immediately brightening. 'Why not?'

She really is marvellous, he thought. What a jammy sod I am. This time I really have landed on the right side.

As they left the dining room, Bill glanced back and shook his head.

## 5

Whenever their ship docked at a new port, Bill was among the first to go ashore, his neck strung about with heavy, old-fashioned cameras like a war correspondent going into action. Helen squinting in front of the Royal Palace in Lisbon, Helen squinting in front of a gilded clocktower in Messina, Helen clinging for dear life to a camel in Petra, while Bill clicked merrily away, whistling some song he felt appropriate: *O Sole Mio, the Sheikh of Araby*, something by Borodin from *The King and I*. Where Carol had left off, Bill now picked up, compiling an imaginary album in which there were no business hiccups, childhood illnesses or family tragedies, just one long calm, cloudless day, at the end of which, standing beside Helen on the terrace overlooking the twinkling port, they enjoyed a cool, reviving cocktail.

Bill was never bored. His mind was too restless for that. Thankfully, for all her success at competitive games, Helen's temper remained astonishingly even. Bill couldn't understand it. However hard she played – at golf, bridge, scrabble, even racing demon – she never got cross, nor confused games with what some sports writers insisted on calling 'real life.'

'It's all very well a bunch of useless bloody politicians telling us what we should or shouldn't think. You only have to watch an Ashes Test from the Sydney Hill, with ockers lobbing beer cans at the English fielders, to know how seriously some people take what the Thought Police call frivolous. Tell that to the Columbian goalie who was shot for letting in a goal at the World Cup. Or those hairy so-called women who represented Iron Curtain countries at the Olympics and are now riddled with cancer from the hormones they were forced to take. Try convincing them sport isn't real life.'

'How's the new swing?' Helen asked.

Like a child, Bill would have liked nothing better than for her to watch him hour after hour whacking golf balls into a net, but she knew she wouldn't have been much use to him.

Having started golf as a child, she'd never tried to analyse what she was doing, trusting her body to make the necessary decisions, and she imagined everyone else must be the same.

'Still coming over the top. Taking the club too much inside. Fanning the face open on the backswing,' he said, shaking his head. 'I can't get rid of my bad habits. Don't suppose I ever shall. I no longer even remember if I'm supposed to supinate or pronate, not that I know what the bloody hell they mean anyway. My first pro got so annoyed with my endless questions that he finally told me, in the nicest possible way, 'to just hit the effing ball... Sir.' Wish I'd listened to him. Now I'm all fouled up in what the Babe called the mechanics of the game.'

'Usually you're so impulsive. I love the way you always say or do the first thing that comes into your head,' Helen said, hoping to console him.

'Without hesitation, deviation or repetition,' he put in, quoting from one of their favourite radio programmes. 'I don't know why either. I mean, I know there are plenty of things I can still do reasonably well,' Bill said, 'yet the only thing I care about is my effing golf swing. Apart from you, of course. In every pro shop some pimply youth is flogging tees who'll never get anywhere in the game yet plays miles better than I ever shall.' Bill looked momentarily thoughtful. 'It's how I value myself, I suppose.'

'Or don't?' Helen hazarded.

'Yes, maybe. You never knew my parents.'

'I'm glad I didn't. They sound horrid.'

'They were, though it pains me to say so.'

'It's permitted.' She smiled.

'I know If anyone else said a word against them I'd be up in arms,' Bill said, mystified by his own contradictions. 'Anyone but you.'

'Only the loved are free,' Helen said, repeating something Pete had told her.

'Someone said that. I wish I could remember who.'

'It's true.'

'Come on,' Bill said, looking like a guilty child, 'let's go and find a nice quiet corner and break open a bottle of bubbly.'

'Yes, let's,' Helen said, taking his hand as his mother never had.

6

Much as he loved his young son, Guy was relieved Alice had taken Luke with her when she'd gone back to Hong Kong. Now he had the tower to himself, he could at last get on with his new show, promised to London for the Spring. It was five years since he'd exhibited anything, and he wondered what people would make of the recent changes. He'd never cared what people thought, even less whether or not they bought anything; other than Pete, that is, whose opinion he valued highly even when they disagreed. Like it or not, there were times one needed someone to bounce ideas off, to question one's subjectivity, to provide some kind of bigger picture. Guy had never aspired to be original. He had worked in a number of styles, derived from the artists he most admired, but had never been a slavish imitator. He had taken only what was useful to him, in technique or point of view; and, even then, wasn't always sure he'd got it right or was doing what the artist himself intended. As if intention was something you were necessarily even aware of. If Guy had known in advance what he was going to achieve, he'd never have started anything – unlike so many contemporary so-called artists who believed the idea alone was sufficient. Luck and accident were as important as any concept or theory, which were only for critics and art historians, the would-be's and never-wasser's who laid down the law without having ever sharpened a pencil. Nowadays, art was just another racket, cooked up by dealers, curators and critics, a gravy train to keep them all employed on inflated salaries at the expense of the jobbing artist. Much like the European Union. The unaccountable in pursuit of the...Guy smiled, taken with the opening of his epigram. The unenviable? The unexpurgated? The undeclared? He knew none of those was quite right, but it would come. If left alone, he knew the *mot juste* would emerge unscathed, like a hound sniffing out truffles in a damp wood. The unconscious was like that. Left it to its own devices, it could always be trusted to come up with the answer. If one was only patient enough, trusting enough.


# 7


'OK Pete, so who's this other woman?' asked Andrea.

'What other woman?'

'The one with the postcards.'

Pete grinned like a naughty schoolboy.

'Oh, you mean Helen?'

'Who's she?'

'Bill's wife. His new wife.'

'Why the fuck's she writing to you?'

'It's from both of them. From their cruise. Pretty dull stuff, to be honest. Take a look,' Pete said. 'See what you're missing.'

'I already did.'

A couple of times a week for the past month, Pete had received a chatty postcard from the happy couple as the *Queen Mary* sailed around the Mediterranean and through the Suez Canal, en route to Colombo. The ship should have gone on to the Far East but had suddenly changed direction and its current destination remained unclear to both passengers and crew.

Pete, who kept an open mind about what he read or heard, assumed it had to do with a virus which was evidently emerging from China; and because little was yet known about it, conspiracy theorists, exploiting the internet, were already having a field day. But whatever the origins of the Coronavirus, whether it had been deliberately started in the Wuhan Institute of Virology or accidentally in the local fish market or, as the Chinese government insinuated, been planted by American servicemen attending the World Military Games in Wuhan the previous year, hundreds of thousands of lives would soon be lost, medical services stretched to breaking point, and economies and societies around the world put under strains unimaginable only moments before.

Under Helen's calming influence, Bill took a surprisingly philosophical view of the crisis, certainly compared to most other passengers, who were running around the ship like headless chickens, while the ever-patient crew and Captain did all they could to reassure them that they were completely safe.

'The vital thing,' Bill told Helen, 'is that we don't stop anywhere or take anyone new on board.'

As soon as he had heard about the virus, Bill began mugging up, and within no time knew more than anyone else on board about previous pandemics, in particular the 1919 Spanish Flu, with which the Coronavirus was already being compared, which had killed more people in two years than died in the entire First World War.

'Give up any thoughts of sightseeing, because there won't be any,' Bill informed his fellow passengers. 'The only safe places were completely isolated from the rest of the world. So if we have to sit it out right here stuffing our faces, so be it.' He glanced around the dining room: 'Could be worse, couldn't it?' he added quietly to Helen.

'Much worse,' she said, resting a consoling hand on his arm.

'Christ I'm glad we didn't do this on the cheap,' he said when they returned to their suite. 'Imagine being stuck below deck in some shabby third-class compartment, surrounded by a load of hopeless bloody Yanks screaming blue murder. Shame we won't be going on to Singapore and Hong Kong. I had some serious treats planned.'

'Next time,' Helen said.

'Yes, next time.'

'You know we'd still have been all right down below,' Helen added. She was unaccustomed to being spoilt and at times found such luxury oppressive, though she'd never have said so to Bill, who had done it all for her.

'You might have been. I always need a bit of space, otherwise I get cabin fever.'

'I look forward to seeing that.'

'No, you don't,' Bill said, vigorously shaking his head. 'Believe me, you really don't.'


8


'What the hell's he doing?' asked Ivan over the phone. He and Pete were having what had become, since Bill's departure, a regular catch-up, but was really no more than an excuse for Ivan to have a good old-fashioned moan about his father.

'Sitting it out on board ship in the lap of luxury, by all accounts.'

'What the fuck for? He should be trying to get home. Doesn't he realise his life's in mortal danger.'

'He wants his money's worth, I expect.'

'Typical! That's so selfish.'

'He says they're as safe there as anywhere else.'

'Bollocks.'

'He believes it.'

'The papers say the virus is out of control and the passengers are dropping like flies.'

'He says there hasn't been a single case on the ship.'

'I don't care what he says.'

'Why not?'

'Anyway, what's the point being a sitting duck on a fucking booze cruise when you can't stop anywhere or see anything?'

'They'll have to stop somewhere. They can't remain at sea forever.'

'That's when it'll get him,' Ivan said, sounding almost triumphant.


9


Having abandoned its original itinerary, the *Queen Mary* stopped at Kuala Lumpur to let off passengers who wanted to go home. Bill and Helen had decided to take pot luck and stick it out on board, for there was talk of sailing to Australia where Bill had always longed to go. Helen knew it well, and had family in Western Australia who, as recipients of her chatty postcards, were already looking forward to meeting her romantic new husband. In the event, it took them almost a month, stopping at Brisbane, Sydney, Melbourne and Adelaide, before the ship finally docked at the most remote city in the world, Perth. From there, a couple of rounds of golf and festive family reunions later, Bill and Helen boarded a packed Emirates Airways flight, arriving in London three days before the first National Lockdown officially began.


'Christ, you cut it fine,' Ivan said, pulling open the front door as Bill fumbled with his keys.

'Go inside, darling,' Bill told Helen. 'I'll settle with the driver.'

'You must be Ivan,' Helen said, smiling as she advanced a hand in greeting. Ivan nodded impassively.

'That's me.'

'Ivan, give your step-mother some help with the bags, will you.'

'Call me Helen, please.'

'Yes, OK,' Ivan said, picking up a suitcase in each hand.

'I don't think your father was expecting you to be here.'

'I'm sure he wasn't.'

'But you're most welcome.'

'Thanks.'

Ivan's first reaction to Helen was unexpectedly favourable, even as he wondered who the fuck she thought she was, inviting him into his own home.

Bill followed them into the house, clambering over the large assortment of suitcases Ivan had dumped haphazardly in the hallway.

'That's not what I mean by giving a hand,' Bill said. 'You might take some of those upstairs.'

'Sorry.'


'So how's tricks?' Bill asked Ivan, when he came back down. Before he could answer, Bill asked Helen if she wanted something to drink. 'I'm parched,' he added.

'A cup of tea would be nice.'

'Good. Fine,' Bill said, not moving from his chair. Helen glanced from Bill to Ivan and back again.

'I'll make it,' she said.

'Something stronger?' Bill asked. Helen shook her head.

'I'll leave you boys alone. What about you, Ivan? Can I get you anything?'

'I'm fine...Thanks.'

'So...' Bill said.

'So what?'

'All OK?' Ivan shrugged.

'Same as everyone else.'

'Worried?'

'Who isn't?'

'Not too terrified, I hope?'

'People your age are the ones who should be. Why aren't you?'

'I've had a pretty good innings. When your time's up, your time's up. How's Mel, by the way?'

Ivan shook his head.

'She's gone.'

'What does that mean?'

'Just that. Look, dad...'

'Yes?'

'I know you weren't expecting me to be here, but is it OK if I crash here for a bit?'

'Do I mind?'

'All right, would Helen mind?'

'Hadn't you better ask her?'

'You're not making this very easy.'

Just giving you a taste of your own medicine, Bill thought.

The door opened and Helen came in carrying a large tray on which sat a highly inviting chocolate cake. Ivan jumped up and cleared a space on the coffee table, then took the tray from her.

'Darling, Ivan wants to know if it's OK for him to camp out here for a bit. I said he should ask you.'

'Of course. It's his home.'

Bill nodded appreciatively.

'I knew you'd say that.'

Yeah, right, Ivan thought, smiling at Helen.

'Then that's settled,' Bill said, not realising what he'd let himself in for.

## 10

'That stuff you talked about the other day,' Pete asked Andrea. 'It wasn't all true? I mean literally. It can't be.'

'Every word. I promise.'

'But why did you never say anything? To your parents. To the police.'

'I was just a kid. No one would have believed me. Not where I come from. Even you didn't believe me.'

'Of course I do. It's just so remote from my own experience.'

'You think I made it up?'

'No, of course not. Maybe elaborated a little here and there. It's what children do. But that's all. What matters is that you believe it.'

Andrea shook her head. Where had Pete been all his life that he couldn't accept that what she'd told him, and him alone, was the God's honest truth?

'Baby,' she said, shaking her head, 'you don't know the half of it.'

## 11

'Coming?' Helen asked, throwing open the bedroom window.

'No thanks. Not today. In fact, never again.'

'Sure?'

'Quite sure.'

It was just before 8pm on a Thursday evening, the hour each week when all over the country people opened wide their windows to applaud the NHS. For the first few weeks of Lockdown, Bill had joined in the clapping, but from the moment he felt it was expected of him, had chosen to opt out. This evening the noise seemed diminished, perhaps reflecting waning enthusiasm for a gesture Bill felt more befitting a tin pot dictatorship than a modern, liberal democracy. But that didn't stop Helen, who waved and beamed at friends and neighbours up and down the tree-lined street. As the noise died away, she closed the window and went and sat beside Bill on the bed.

'You didn't mind?' he asked, taking her hand.

'Not in the least. I only do it out of habit, not wanting to be seen doing the wrong thing. I've always been like that.'

Bill patted her hand.

'There's sure to be some sneak out there scanning the street for shirkers.' Bill made an obscene gesture towards the window.

'It makes me so proud, the way this lockdown has brought us closer together,' Helen said.

'I didn't think we could be any closer.'

'All of us. The whole country.'

'Ah, the old Dunkirk spirit. Or is it the Blitz? I can never remember.'

'Don't joke. What's important is it's happening.'

'If you say so.'

'I mean it. This could be the start of something new and wonderful, way beyond politics, a radical re-evaluation of values and priorities for all of us.'

'Somehow I doubt it. In no time it'll be business as usual.'

'Nothing will ever be the same again.'

'You don't honestly believe that?'

Helen nodded.

'You're just an old cynic,' she said.

Bill shook his head, but when he tried to pat her hand again, he felt her pull away.

'No, darling. Just a realist.'

Bill and Helen rarely discussed politics: by nature she was a peacemaker, whereas he resembled a naughty child throwing fireworks into a crowded room, wanting to provoke a reaction yet frightened when there was one. That they held different views on a whole range of subjects did not seem to bother either of them, or put a damper on their mutual devotion, something that could not be said of too many families in the UK at that especially difficult time.

'As usual, the government's got it arse over tit', Bill said, 'putting protecting the NHS before saving peoples' lives, which you'd think was the whole point of the sacred bloody cow. Sacred cash cow, more like. Lord knows who they're using, but if I'd been running this campaign...'

Some years earlier, Bill had briefly worked for the government, masterminding a campaign to increase awareness of prostate cancer among middle-aged men, something previous administrations had always shied away from. 'Fifty pence a head, that's all it would have cost to test every bloke in the country, and they still refused to cough up. Yet when it comes to women and breast cancer the cheque book is always open. Why do you think that is?' But before Helen could answer, Bill went on: 'It's because most men die with it, so they don't feel any need to buy their votes. That's why.'

'What's that got to do with the price of eggs?'

'Nothing really. Just blowing off steam.'

'You don't believe a word of that, do you? Not seriously.'

'Let's have a drink,' Bill said, offering up his favourite panacea for pretty much any problem.

For a month now the UK had been in almost total lockdown. Schools and universities, pubs and restaurants, cinemas and theatres, most shops and offices, places of worship, museums and galleries, sporting venues large and small, indoor and out, all had been shut, irrespective of the risk to heath or impact on the country's economy. Except for an hour's daily exercise, no social life was permitted outside the home, though many better-off people, regarding themselves as exceptions to any rule, snuck off to the country where they felt free to moan about intolerable attacks on individual liberty.

'When will these bloody people realise it has nothing to do with being grown up enough to decide whether or not to go to the pub, but with stopping the spread of this infernal virus,' Bill said to Pete, who had slipped out under cover of darkness to spend the evening with his old friend. They were watching the Prime Minister's nightly address to the nation, while upstairs Helen was playing on-line bridge and Ivan was Skyping Mel.

'Andrea doesn't mind you coming here?'

'Why would she? She's delighted to have me out of the way for a bit so she can wallow in her own personal space. Ommmmmmmmm,' Pete added, imitating the old Hippie chant.

'Peace and love bruv,' Bill said, making a Churchillian V sign.

'I'm amazed she puts up with me. I mean, I'm not the easiest person to live with and the flat's pretty small.'

'She's no picnic.'

'Indeed not.'

Pete glanced at Bill. 'Have you ever regretted...?' His sentence was unfinished but both knew what he was referring to.

'Not for a millisecond. Not since meeting Helen, anyway.'

'Would you like to see her again?'

Bill shook his head.

'Not a great idea.'

'It just seems odd, me always coming here on my own, or talking to her about Helen, who she's never met.'

'Why do you need to talk about Helen?'

'I don't.'

'Then please don't.'

'OK.'

Bill smiled.

'One day maybe, but not yet. OK?'

'Yes, OK. One day.'

## 12

'Technology's completely altered the way we react to events,' Bill told Pete. 'We see all this carnage on TV, bombings and mass killings, and think if they were only a bit more like us and managed their affairs better, none of this shit would happen. We hear about migrant boats sinking in the Med and riots in refugee camps, and the French blithely shoving them all on to us, people who want to come here more than anywhere in the whole effing world, the very same people we've been suggesting should behave more like us. Yet as soon as they try, risking their lives and their families to cross the mighty ocean just to get to dear old Blighty, we say sorry chum, not on your nelly, bugger off back to whatever Godforsaken hole you've crept out of. And you know what the worst thing about it is?'

'Go on,' Pete said.

'The worst thing is that I'm one of those bloody Brits who wishes the whole sodding lot would just eff off back to wherever they come from and stop bothering me. When in truth they don't bother me at all. I mean, not in the bloody least. But because the effing BBC think they have a duty to rake up all this miserable shit and dump it on my doorstep, they make it my problem.'

'It's the old global village,' Pete said. 'They're never dumped anywhere near you or me. Instead, the Home Office or Border Farce, whichever useless lot it is, make bloody sure it's one of those hideous post-industrial hell-holes oop north, where they can be guaranteed a full British welcome. And we then wonder why the ungrateful sods want to blow us all up.'

'And because it's all we ever see or hear about on TV, apart from Celebrity Farting or some daft food programme watched devotedly by zillions who've never cooked a meal in their lives, I'm told it's my problem, even when I know it isn't. D'you follow?'

'Sort of.'

'Helen would've given up ages ago.'

'I don't blame her.'

Bill stood up and stumbled towards the drinks tray. They had been hard at it all evening, ever since the golf on TV had finished, and Pete was struggling to stay awake.

'Another?' Bill asked over his shoulder. Pete nodded.

'I may have to crash on your sofa.'

'Be my guest.'

'Mustn't risk being stopped by Her Majesty's Constabulary and asked why I'm not tucked up in in my own bloody bed.'

'Never succumb to the forces of law and order. In no time we'll be living in a police state.'

'According to some dim-witted Supreme Court judge we already are.'

'I've no time for judges. They know fuck-all about the real world.'

Bill cocked his chin towards the kitchen. 'Helen's made us some sandwiches, the sweetheart. She's in the final of some tournament on Zoom and mustn't be disturbed. Told me not to wait up, but the thing is, I can't sleep if she isn't right next to me, so she'll probably find me spark out beside you on the bloody sofa and get all the wrong ideas, and if she wakes me up I'll get all cross and it'll be tears before bedtime, well breakfast, any- way. God, I hate myself sometimes,' Bill added, shaking his head.

'She and Ivan seem to be getting on all right,' Pete said.

'Thick as bloody thieves, they are.'

'That must cheer you up.'

'Why?'

'It's what you want, isn't it?'

Bill plonked their drinks down onto the coffee table.

'Oops. Sorry. What did you say?'

'I said isn't that what you want? Ivan and Helen getting along well.'

'Is it?' Bill said. 'Sometimes I think it's the last bloody thing I want. The way the virus is going I, I mean we, may never get rid of the sanctimonious little shit. It's like living with the bloody Stasi. Ever since this bloody lockdown began I can't take a piss without feeling under surveillance.'

'It can't be that bad.'

'It's worse.'

'What does he want?'

'Search me. Before we went away, the little bastard wanted me dead, well maybe not literally dead but somewhere conveniently out of the way, as if all of this...' Bill made a sweeping gesture which took in the entire room, the entire house, 'was already his.'

'It's called entitlement syndrome. Believing someone else's property belongs to you.'

Bill appeared perplexed. Then he broke into a broad grin.

'You just made that up, didn't you. You must have.'

'Only the name. The syndrome is real enough. Carol could have explained it far more fully.'

'Yes, well. She doesn't have to deal with the effing fallout.'

## 13

Despite being stuck at home all week, Bill and Helen saw less of each other than before the lockdown. That hadn't been agreed, or even discussed, but both had things to do which seemed to fill their time, and apart from passing on the stairs, or popping a head round the door, it was only at meal-times or in front of the TV that they spent any continuous time together. Most of the day Helen stayed upstairs, reading whodunnits and playing bridge on line, while straight after breakfast each morning Bill slipped out of the house, Leica concealed in his saddlebag, and peddled into town, determined to record London under lockdown in all its unique emptiness, bereft of people and traffic, as if after a neutron bomb. He wasn't sure how the idea had come to him, or even if it had originally been his; and would occasionally see someone else with much the same idea, taking similar advantage of the solitude and quiet.

After lunch, if the weather was fine, he and Helen would stroll on Wimbledon Common, Bill employing a 9 iron as a walking stick with which, when the coast was clear, he would chip golf balls. Between then and dinner he would watch *Shell's Wonderful World of Golf* or old British Opens on You-Tube, mimicking the deadpan commentary of his beloved Henry Longhurst while putting on the carpet.

Ivan could not disguise his disapproval. He felt his father should be following the rules as they were written, not as he chose to loosely interpret them: an hour's exercise a day was all that was permitted, and shopping only for essentials. As for Pete regularly popping in, if it had been anyone else Ivan would have given his father a piece of his mind. Whether he genuinely feared for his father, or just needed someone on whom to focus his rage at being separated from Mel, remained open to question. Unsurprisingly, Helen favoured the former interpretation. Although Ivan was very much a presence in the house, he preferred to eat alone in his room or use the kitchen when they had finished with it, or to go for a solitary run or bike ride. He never offered to do any shopping, and evidently expected his laundry to be done for him. But Helen chose to say nothing. Ironing gave her something different to do when bored and household chores had never bothered her. If anything, she found them relaxing.

'You don't seem worried,' Helen said to Bill, one morning over breakfast. As usual, Ivan was sleeping late. He rarely came downstairs before lunchtime.

'What about?'

'About Ivan.'

'Should I be?'

'It isn't natural for someone his age to spend so much time on his own.'

'There's nothing I can do about that. It's hardly my fault.'

'No one says it is.'

'He makes me feel it is.'

'Not really. He's just angry at the world.'

'Who isn't?'

Helen appeared surprised.

'You seem as happy as Larry. Positively thriving, if you ask me.'

'You shouldn't always judge by appearances.'

'I never judge.'

'Sorry I spoke.'

'We all get a bit edgy at times. It isn't your fault.'

'I know that.'

'Why not have a talk with him?' she said.

'He knows where I am.'

'I mean a proper talk.'

'What about?'

'Anything. Just to communicate. For God's sake Bill, you're his father.'

'Thanks for reminding me.'


## 14

'What is it with you Brits and Christmas?' Andrea asked.

It was early July, the Lockdown had at last been lifted, and on a glorious summer morning she and Pete were lounging on a terrace overlooking the Seine, drinking pastis.

'God's an Englishman. Don't you know that?'

'What are you talking about? Jesus was the King of the Jews.'

'The two aren't mutually exclusive. At least we don't think so.' Pete smiled, but when Andrea didn't respond as he had hoped, he suddenly became nervous. 'I'm joking.'

'We don't joke about our Saviour.'

'I thought that was your President,' Pete said, unable to stop himself. 'Or maybe he just thinks he's God.'

'There you go again,' she said shaking her head. 'Always with the jokes. Pete, don't you believe in anything?'

Religion and politics: two subjects to be avoided at all costs, he reminded himself, especially with Americans.

'OK, where shall I start? Rembrandt, Uccello, Bach, Evelyn Waugh, Maurice Gee.'

'Maurice Who?'

'My favourite novelist. Janáček, the Beatles. Hein van de Geyn. He's a bass player. Schubert. Johnny Hartman. Giorgio Morandi. My favourite painter.'

Andrea held up her hands.

'Enough already! I believe you.'

But Pete was into his stride, and not even Andrea could stop him now. 'Don Bradman. Bobby Jones.'

'The golfer?' Pete smiled, delighted she had heard of him. 'He came from Atlanta too.'

'Maybe the most interesting man who ever lived, certainly the first person I'd invite to my all-time dinner party. Orson Welles, Mozart, though neither of them would know when to shut up. Not too many women, I'm afraid, but you won't mind that. Gwen John would never say a word. Jean Rhys would flirt with all the men. Mavis Gallant. Elizabeth Taylor – the writer not the actress. Peggy Lee. A fruitcake, but she can always sing for her supper. Charles Darwin. Richard Cromwell. Christopher Wren. Chekhov. Handel. William Hazlitt. The evidence of my own eyes and ears. Jesus Christ, but only on a good day. He could always do the catering!'

'Pete, you can't say things like that.'

'How am I doing?'

'Don't you take anything I say seriously?'

'I take everything seriously. You must know that.'


'I don't get it,' Andrea said a little later. 'Your government treats you like shit, tells you unless you behave properly

Christmas will be cancelled, and you just roll over. Where I come from...'

'I know all about where you come from. Where a virgin is someone who can run faster than her uncle.'

'Her sister. Only I didn't have one.'

'Sorry. I shouldn't have said that.'

'It's OK. Ever since I dumped all that stuff on you, I've felt a whole lot better.'

'It's good to get things off your chest.' Even if, Pete added to himself, the chest isn't entirely yours.

As soon as the National Lockdown had ended, Andrea and Pete had jumped into her swish silver sports car and driven to France. Andrea loved to drive, the faster the better, yet Pete, who had never owned a car and had always been a nervous passenger, seemed not to mind.

'Did your uncle also teach you to drive?'

'My brother.'

'Normally, I keep my eyes firmly shut. But with you I feel safe. Strange.'

'Why wouldn't you? I'm a great driver.'

'Habit, I expect. Like you, I don't trust easily. I always need proof in advance.'

'There ain't no such thing. That's why you got to have faith.'

'Faith in what?'

'The good Lord. Or maybe just good sex...'

'Hallelujah! I'm a believer!'

Hand in hand, they strolled along the quayside, then crossed the river and found an old-fashioned bistro, with red and white tablecloths and matching cane chairs, and supercilious-waiters deliberately neglecting their customers.

'How long do we have?' Andrea asked, when their order had finally been taken. Pete glanced at his watch. 'I mean, when's Guy expecting us?'

'He said it didn't matter. He's not going anywhere. He never goes anywhere these days.'

'No hurry then?'

'None whatsoever.'

'Great. Because I have this cute idea.'

'What kind of idea?'

'It's a surprise.'

'I don't like surprises.'

'Yeah, I know. For once you're going to have to be patient.'


Feeling mellow after lunch, they wandered back towards their hotel, past the burnt-out shell of Notre Dame and down shaded streets with narrow, uneven pavements, crammed with antique shops and art galleries and Parisians who refused to give way. Pressed against a shop window, Andrea said: 'I used to love all this junk. Buying stuff like it was going out of style. Doing up other folks houses and spending all their money. Now I don't want any of it.'

'That's because you've got me.'

'I guess so.'

They walked on, then stopped in front of a gallery full of garish oil paintings. Shaking his head, Pete said: 'It makes me want to cry. When I think how hard it is for young artists to make a living, and all we ever see is this unspeakable shit.'

'How do they stay in business when you never see anyone in them?'

Pete shrugged. It was a thought which had never occurred to him. 'Maybe they're a front,' Andrea suggested.

'You mean for more shit?'

'Yeah, right.'

'You know,' Pete said, taking Andrea's hand, 'over the years I've had a few really gifted students. Not many, but enough to make me feel my job wasn't a complete waste of time. Once in a while someone still gets in touch to tell me what they're doing, and how grateful they are for what I taught them, and I never know how to respond, because I didn't think I was doing anything really. I'm pleased, don't get me wrong, but all I ever did, or tried to do, was to get them to use their own eyes, to see for themselves. Nowadays no one seems to have a clue what's real and what isn't.'

'We're for real, you and me. You know that?' Pete nodded.

'Most of the time. There's an English expression: those who can do. Those who can't, teach. That seems a pretty apt description of me. I once thought I might have something interesting to say.'

'You still do... Everybody does.'

'No, I don't. I'm not sure I ever did. Not anything original, anyway. It's only taken me half a century to find that out.'

'That's really sad.'

'No, it's not. And you know something else?'

'Go ahead, Mr Modesty. Tell me. I really want to know.'

'I no longer give a shit. I care about you more than I ever

thought I would about anyone. But as for all that other stuff I once worried myself silly about, ambition and success and making my mark on the world, frankly it's a relief to know that, compared to this, none of that matters.'

## 15

'I can't remember ever feeling this nervous before a match,' Bill told Helen, his partner in the long-postponed final of the Mixed Winter Foursomes. They were standing on the pro shop steps, waiting for a pair on the tee to drive off. It was eight weeks since Bill had been at the golf club and he had been dreading this day, ceaselessly rehearsing their forthcoming match and obsessing over whether it would be better for Helen to play the odds or evens.

'I'd be more worried if you weren't,' she said. 'A certain amount of tension's just what the doctor ordered. Can't have you too relaxed.' She smiled reassuringly, but for once he appeared unpersuaded.

'I only wish I was.'

To distract himself, Bill went inside and bought one of the fancy new ball markers engraved with the club logo which he superstitiously imagined might up his game.

'D'you know which I'm meant to play off? Whites or yellows? he asked Helen. 'I assume you're off the Ladies.'

'Darling, you're out of date. There are no Men's or Ladies' tees. We're all the same now.'

'Which do the trannies play from?'

Helen smiled.

'It's just different colours, to go with this new handicapping system they're bringing in from America.'

'Yankee imperialism by another name. If it isn't broke, why fix it?'

'When did you last play to your handicap? I know I can't regularly.'

'I never can, but that isn't the point. It's meant to represent you at your best. An ideal you, if you like. It's like the difference between taking an exam and continuous assessment, where the parents do their kids homework and get all the answers from Google. What kind of a test is that?'

'Not now, darling. You should be warming up.'

But Bill had the bone between his teeth, and was not to be diverted, even by this woman he adored.

'There'll always be cheats and bandits. They come with the territory. But why punish the poor old 18 handicapper who's the backbone of every club? Typical bloody Yanks to think they can eliminate the element of chance. What the fuck do they think life is?'

'They say the new system will be fairer.'

'Fairer to whom?'

'To everyone. Wherever you play, you'll have a handicap measured against the difficulty of the course.'

'All courses are bloody difficult, as far as I'm concerned.'

'Not today. Not with me as your partner,' Helen said, squeezing his hand. 'Trust me. You'll be fine. As long as you do as I say.'

Bill knew she was right. He was only banging on because he was feeling nervous, and terrified of letting her down.

'Of course I trust you. It's me I'm not so sure about.'

'You'll be fine,' she repeated. 'Now do your stretches while I hit off. And whatever the result, no apologies. I know you're doing your best.'

'Righto, Skip,' Bill said, clicking his heels.


To the frustration of golfers everywhere, courses and club-houses had been closed for much of the lockdown. In perfect weather the general public had roamed at will across fairway and green, their children capering in the sand, while crows and moles went merrily about their business. For seven weeks, to anyone who would listen, Bill had been decrying government policy for encouraging exercise while at the same banning its most effective and popular forms.

'It's yet more social bloody engineering,' he had sounded off to Pete more than once. 'They can't afford to alienate the so-called Red Wall, so are playing the class card, which is how most of them think of golf anyway. As a bloody toffs' game. Which of course is bollocks. Golf is for everyone.'

'I don't remember too many black faces at your club,' Pete had said.

'I assume you're referring to 'people of colour?' That's only because they don't play. We've Indian doctors and Chinese dentists, and even a distinguished Sinhalese silk who's black as your hat, plus any number of Jewish accountants and so-licitors. Even some black cab drivers we let in when we were short of readies. So everyone, really, from all walks of life. A genuine multicultural melting pot.'

'Honestly?'

'Absolutely. Just like the effing UN.'

## 16

'Darling, you were brilliant, absolutely brilliant,' Helen said, as they sat in the smoke room celebrating victory. 'So confident. So cool under pressure. My parfit gentil Knight.'

Bill put on a modest face.

'Only because of you, my love. I didn't want to let you down.'

'You never do.'

'I must admit that was a pretty good chip of mine on 13,' Bill said.

'It turned the match. At that point it could have gone either way.'

'And how about my bunker shot on 9?'

Helen shook her head.

'I should never have put you in there.'

Bill glowed.

'Bunkers hold no terrors for old pros like me.'

'I knew I could count on you.'

'What about your glorious tee shot on 5,' Bill said. 'I thought it was going in.'

'For a blissful moment so did I!'

'How lucky we are,' he said, raising his glass.

'More than lucky. Blessed.'

<br>

17

'What a view!' Pete exclaimed, gazing south towards the Pyrenees from the roof of Guy's tower. Beneath them, the valley was shrouded in early morning mist, but on the horizon brilliant shafts of sunlight were beginning to break through, like something in a medieval miniature.

'I hear the sound of battle down below,' Guy said. 'Men in armour happily hacking each other to bits.'

'There's a cheerful thought to start the day! I can see why you don't want to come back.'

'I couldn't live anywhere else.'

'I don't blame you.'

'One night years ago I saw a bonfire burning over there,' Guy said, pointing across the valley. 'It made me think of ancient encampments, Roman soldiers trying to keep warm in their bivouacs, that sort of sentimental tosh. The next day I saw the bloody farmers had cut down all the lovely old trees and hedgerows to enlarge their fields. That taught me never to romanticise the countryside.'

They stood in silence as the sun rose, contemplating the landscape. Pete asked after Alice, whom he had still to meet.

'She hated it here. She thinks the French are all racists, which of course they are, but probably no worse than anywhere else, they're just more upfront about it. And she's worried about what's happening in Hong Kong. She's very into family.'

'Why aren't you family?'

Guy shrugged.

'She's very Chinese.'

'What about Luke?'

'I miss him terribly. She's obsessed with sending him to a proper English Public School, which I've done everything to discourage. But it's no good. I never get anywhere.' Pete raised his eyebrows. 'I'll wait and see what she decides.'

Wanting to change the subject, Guy asked Pete if he'd been to look at the Marquets in Bordeaux.

'They aren't on view. They now keep them in a basement. He's rather out of fashion.'

'He was never in fashion. That's what I love about him. You can't quite see how he brings it off. Same with Morandi.'

Pete nodded.

'Lots of turps, I expect!' Pete smiled. 'It's their singlemindedness, the way they convey their vision through the paint itself. We've all tried the same tricks, but it doesn't usually work. Without the self-belief, I mean.' Pete glanced at Guy. 'You have it. I've always known that. It's one of the reasons you're so good. I've at last accepted that I don't, which in a way is a relief. It means I can stop pretending. Those who can do...'

Guy shook his head. 'God, you're so bloody British. Stop putting yourself down.'

'It's what I am. I don't have any choice.'

'We all have choice.'

When Andrea had finished her toilette, they drove into town to the weekly market. Pete accompanied Guy from stall to stall while Andrea trailed behind, trying on scarves and hats.

'How do I look?' she said, doing a twirl before the two men.

'Great,' Pete said.

'Too big,' Guy said, studying her carefully. 'That hat makes you look shorter than you are.'

'Gee, thanks.'

'Don't worry about him,' Pete said, when Guy had moved away. 'I think it looks terrific. As always.'

'Well, thank you, kind sir,' she said, curtseying. 'He's weird.'

'Not really. Just serious.'

'*So* intense.' Pete nodded. 'But as I know you like him,' she added, taking his arm. 'I better had too.'

'Not just for my sake.'

'For both our sakes.'


After lunch, tired after the long drive, Pete took a nap. When he woke there was no one about, so he went up to the roof, hoping to spot Andrea and Guy. By the time they eventually returned, it was almost dark and Pete was into his second whisky.

'I was worried,' he said, feeling uncomfortably far from Andrea.

'You figured the big bad wolf got me, huh?' She embraced him warmly, then suddenly pulled away.

'Pete, you didn't? You couldn't?'

'Didn't what?'

'You didn't think...?'

Pete shrugged.

'It wouldn't be the first time.'

'What the fuck does that mean?'

He was remembering his first lunch with Andrea, when she had been about to marry Bill, and their ecstatic afternoon in bed together.

'It doesn't matter.'

'Sure it does. What the hell's eating you?'

'I missed you, that's all. When I woke up I wasn't sure where I was.'

'Not that again?'

'I was disorientated. I wanted you here.'

'I'm here now.'

'It was stupid of me. I'm sorry.'

She took his hands and stared into his eyes.

'Pete, sometimes you gotta have faith,' she said, drinking from his glass.


## 18


'That surprise you mentioned the other day. You never said what it was,' Pete told Andrea a couple of days later on the drive back to Paris.

'Didn't I?'

'You know you didn't.'

She smiled slyly.

'Be patient. I'm not quite there yet.'

'You're just teasing me.'

Andrea briefly took her eyes off the road to look at Pete.

'Trust me. It'll be worth waiting for. Now go back to sleep.'


## 19


'How's Ivan doing?' Pete asked Bill

He had parked his bike at Bill's house, and as they walked across Wimbledon Common towards the Fox & Grapes, Bill took regular nips from a hip flask which he proffered to Pete, who shook his head.

'Spoils of victory?'

'Another day, another trophy! Smart, isn't it?'

The silver-plated flask was engraved with crossed golf clubs and the date of Bill's heroics. 'All on my tod for once, though Helen's encouragement undoubtedly put lead in my pencil. She kept telling me to play my natural game, whatever that is, and it paid off in spades. The enemy was not so much defeated as crushed.' He took another swig and again offered the flask to Pete. 'Funny, I never imagined love could be so...'

'Liberating?'

'Precisely.'

'Me too. I always believed one plus one made less than two. That's why I didn't marry for so long. What politicians call an issue of trust.'

When they were sitting down, Pete asked after Ivan, who had recently picked up the Coronavirus at the school where he was teaching, and was now self-isolating with Bill and Helen.

'She says he's over the worst, thank God, because I didn't want him near any hospital. Bloody death traps.'

Looking unusually thoughtful, Bill rested his chin on his beer glass.

'Funny to think of all those weeks in lockdown when I felt under house arrest, with Ivan ordering me around like Rosa Kleb. In my own bloody home, for God's sake! A nightmare vision of what it must feel to be stuck away in a care home. When the staff aren't humouring you, they're nicking all your stuff, and if you complain they pretend you've lost your marbles. Classic Hitchcock territory.'

'Wonderful lady, Helen.'

'As usual, she was the first to spot anything. He just thought he had a bad cold. When he said he'd no sense of smell, I thought lucky you, not having to taste any more of that dreadful muck Mel feeds him.'

'I thought they'd split up.'

'Three months apart seems to have done them the world of good. She now looks almost normal. Not getting to a hairdresser, I suppose. She got rid of that dreadful purple mop as well as all those bits of shrapnel sticking out of her face. Her parents had something to do with that, I expect.'

'I very much doubt it. I like her. She stops Ivan taking himself too seriously.'

'I wish! D'you remember at the start of the pandemic all those middle-class cunts airily saying, as if they were in Harrods, Ooh, I'll have just a small dose please, if you don't mind, enough to provide a little immunity?' Pete grinned. 'It's amazing how many supposedly intelligent people refused to take it seriously. Still don't. Advertising used to be full of Oxbridge know-alls like Cameron without an ounce of common sense. And in those days a bloody degree meant something.'

'I was convinced I'd die if I ever caught it,' Pete said. 'But after a bit I suddenly stopped worrying. I went on doing everything we were told, still do, washing my hands all the time and not touching door handles, and wearing a mask in shops and buses and avoiding crowded places, but it was like living in a parallel universe. Every evening there was that same panel of glum faces on TV, with their endless bloody charts and graphs, and dire warnings and pious hopes for some miracle test or vaccine, anything to get them off the hook, yet none of it felt real.'

'That's because we never actually see anyone die. Sometimes I think I must be in the wrong place.' Bill shook his head. 'I mean, I've always felt that a bit about myself. You always seemed to know exactly where you were.'

'It was the last thing I felt.'

'I shouldn't say this, especially with Ivan still not being one hundred percent, but I really enjoyed the lockdown, even under his dictatorship. Over all, I'd say it's been the single most interesting period of my entire life, the first universal shared experience I've ever been through.'

'Like a war, you mean?'

Bill nodded.

'I couldn't agree more.'

'It is a bloody war, only against an unseen enemy. Or so we keep being told.'

'As all future wars will be.'

'All the big political events of my life: the Iron Curtain, the Cuban Missile Crisis, Czechoslovakia, Viet Nam, terrorism, the Twin Towers, Sarajevo, the death of Communism, what some dumb Yank called the End of History – all of it seemed to be happening somewhere offstage. But this virus is entirely different. It feels like being invaded by Martians.'

'I sometimes think Ivan was dropped here from outer space, he's so unlike anyone I know. Like Superman arriving from Bizarro.'

'Krypton.'

'Wherever.'

'The main thing is, even if he doesn't know how to express it, he cares deeply about you. The way you do about him,' Pete said.

For a while Bill appeared lost in thought. Then he said: 'I'd never wish this bloody virus on anybody, least of all my own flesh and blood, you know that. But when it's all over it will be no bad thing if the young at last accept that they're mortal too, just like the bloody rest of us, and that contrary to popular belief there's really no such thing as a free lunch.'

'Honestly, Bill!' Pete said, shaking his head

## 20

'Bill's in a state,' Pete told Andrea. 'He pretends there's nothing to worry about, but I can tell he's terrified for Ivan. He was the same with Carol. Couldn't stop telling her what to do to beat the cancer, and all because he felt so helpless. Thank God for Helen. He'd be lost without her, and he knows it.'

'Lucky Bill,' Andrea said, flatly.

'Lucky me, don't you mean?'

'Lucky us.'

'Yes, lucky us.'

## 21

As winter approached, life returned to something resembling normality, even as the pundits kept insisting that life after Coronavirus could never be the same: like the poor, the virus would always be with us. Bill, who had been saying much the same all along, at last felt vindicated, though it provided little consolation as no one appeared to be listening. Covid 19, he insisted, was a wake-up call exposing the fragility not just of our antiquated institutions – Parliament, the NHS, Border Force, the legal system, the universities, education, the police, whatever – but of Parliamentary Democracy itself. Compared to authoritarian regimes more adept at combating the virus, western liberalism was sluggish and inefficient, its politicians terrified of taking decisions, which they instead handed over to so-called experts who, needing to appear omniscient, confused personal opinion with observable fact. And then, as the weather worsened and the predicted second wave arrived, those same authoritarian regimes suddenly seemed rather less efficient than had been assumed by proponents of governmental control; indeed, it hardly seemed to matter what steps were now taken to control the disease, when populations the world over were increasingly reluctant to do as they were told – without which, there was a cat's chance in hell of the virus ever being contained, let alone overcome.

Faced with such uncertainty Ivan, now more or less recovered, took his future in both hands and proposed marriage to Mel.

'If Dad can do it, so can I,' he told Pete, over the phone.

'You're not doing it for him, I hope?' Pete asked.

'Not bloody likely. I love Mel and she loves me.'

'That's wonderful.'

'She saved my life. I didn't want to frighten the old bastard, but I was a lot sicker than he thought. Helen didn't tell him because she knew he'd only go into a tailspin, same as he did with Mum. He's hopeless when he's not in control.'

'But you're OK now?'

'I don't have much energy, so can't exercise the way I like, but hopefully it'll soon come back.'

'Take up golf. That's not too energetic.'

'Mel would love that. She'd never get to see me.'

'I mean it. I used to think it was just a lot of old farts in stupid clothes, but it isn't. It's a metier, and a rather fascinating one. All about your relationship with yourself.'

'You're joking?'

'I promise.'

'Next you'll be suggesting I play with the old man.'

'You could do a lot worse.'

'Honestly Pete! You listen to him far too much.'

'Not at all. For once I've been listening to myself.'


## 22


'Bloody good sausages,' Bill told Pete, wiping his ketchup-covered fingers on a paper napkin. 'You can't beat the great British banger. 100% pure pork. None of your bleedin' halal here, mate.'

'Plus some added breadcrumbs. Otherwise they'd taste too meaty.'

'And with any luck contravening – don't you love that word, the way it rolls off the tongue – some bloody EU regulation or other.' Bill took a deep breath, then exhaled, sending tiny bits of gristle flying across the teak table. 'I bloody well hope so. Bangers and mash. Worcester sauce. Jellied eels. Lancashire hot pot. Blue Stilton. The Austin Mini. Makes one proud to be British.'

The two men were sitting on the terrace outside the halfway house, gazing down the tenth hole. It was one of those sublime late autumn afternoons, when the sun had set low over the russet woods, casting deep shadows across the fairways, and revealing all the insidious humps and bumps to which golfers are blind in broad daylight.

'This is my favourite view,' Bill said, echoing the sentiment inscribed on the back of his bench. 'I can think of worse places to die.'

'It'll be sooner than you think if you eat that second sausage,' Pete said.

'Don't tell Helen. She's trying to get me to lose weight.'

'She doesn't want to be a widow again.'

'I'm not that fat,' Bill said, snapping his waistband as he held in his stomach. 'If I am it's because I'm happy. She can't have it both ways.'

'I took your advice,' Pete said, smiling.

'About the new Ping putter? It'll knock strokes off your score, I guarantee.'

'About getting divorced.'

'I didn't think you were married.'

'From Sarah.'

'Who? Oh, her. I thought that was done and dusted ages ago.'

'There didn't seem much point until now.'

'Why now?'

'I want to marry Andrea.'

'Jesus!'

'You don't mind, I hope.'

'Why should I?'

'You once wanted to marry her. Sorry, twice!'

'That was before I met Helen. She changed everything. A bit like these new handicaps.'

'You don't have to put in cards to her, I hope?'

'Not yet!'

The winter sun ducked behind the trees and suddenly the fairway was invisible.

'I hate it when it's like this,' Bill said, getting to his feet. Fiddling with his face mask, he went inside the half-way house, returning with two large paper cups.

'I almost forgot these,' he said, banging them down on the table.

'How was the wedding?' Pete asked.

'Great. I mean, as great as any wedding can be when only half a dozen people are permitted. They're planning a big do in the Spring, if regulations allow. At her parents' gaff.'

'Hardly a gaff. It's an effing palace.'

'You'd never know it, I mean from meeting her. She's a sweet little thing.'

'She's not a thing, Bill, she's a person.'

'Christ, you sound just like Ivan.'

'He has to take after someone.'

'You know,' Bill said, struggling with the cover to his drink, 'when the first lockdown started I thought it was the end for golf clubs, they'd all go bust. But the opposite turned out to be true.'

'The law of unintended consequences.'

'Courses have never been busier, and we've even got a waiting list. First time in years. I had a hell of a job getting Ivan in before they closed the membership. For once I took your advice and pulled rank.'

'Good for you.'

'You can have too much bloody democracy, especially in golf clubs. Benevolent dictatorship is what they need.'

'There's no such thing.'

'That's just what the son and heir said.'

'I meant to ask, where are they going to live?'

'Didn't I tell you? We've made the house over to them. It's far too big for us, and anyway, it holds too many memories. I want a fresh start. We're moving to Aldeburgh.'

'You're not serious?'

'Helen has a brother up there who's a member of the golf club and he's promised to get me in. Her name is on the honours board for winning some county championship when she was still in nappies.'

'Lovely churches in that part of the world. Knapped flint.'

'So Helen tells me. The club's full of retired spooks. A bit too much bloody gorse for my liking.'

'What are you going to do? I mean, it's the middle of nowhere.'

'Helen's very musical, so there's the festival. And I love oysters.'

'Is that all?'

'I may never have told you, but I've always wanted to do a book on links courses. I know Aldeburgh isn't strictly a links, but it's as good as, and with my photography, I can combine the two.'

'I hope you have more success than me with my Suffolk churches.'

'We could do it together. My snaps and your sketches.'

'Andrea has other plans for me.'

159

'Why am I not surprised?'

'She thinks I need something meaningful to do.'

'To keep you off the golf course?'

'She's had it up her sleeve for some time. When we were in France she talked it over with Guy, who's come into some money from his mum, and they've come up with some hair-brained scheme to set up a not-for-profit arts foundation on the internet, to promote promising young artists, with muggins here in charge.' Pete shook his head. 'For a moment I thought there was something going on between them, they were so bloody furtive. She has all this bread, and because of something tactless I once said, has decided to do something useful with it.'

'No more plastic surgery then?'

'I like her just as she is.'

'I don't blame you. It doesn't sound such a stupid idea, either. You can't play golf all the time.'

'You do.'

'You're not me.'

The course was now in darkness and even their trolleys, parked only a few feet away, were invisible. The student running the half-way house began to clear the tables of discarded sauce sachets and screwed-up napkins and masks, the familiar detritus elderly golfers habitually leave behind.

'Sorry gents, but I've got to close up.'

Lifting their paper cups, Bill and Pete made room for him to wipe the table.

'Don't worry about us,' Bill said. 'We'll just sit here for a bit contemplating the view.'

'But you can't see anything.'

'Oh yes we can.'

'Suit yourselves. Careful on your way back. The path's slippery.'

'Tell me about it,' Bill said.


The lights went out in the half-way house and the sound of a golf buggy faded into the night.

'Kids?'

'A bloody menace. What about them?'

'Ivan and Mel. Are they planning to have any? I always took her for one of those well-intentioned loonies who thought the only way of saving the planet was to kill off the whole human race.'

'She'd have a job doing that, the way our Muslim brothers procreate. We've already lost that battle. In 50 years' time it'll be bloody Sharia law. But at least it won't be my problem.'

'No more sausages in golf clubs.'

'No more golf clubs period. Just tented bloody villages. By the way, have you heard the latest bit of madness from our beloved London mayor. He wants to move the town hall to Islamabad.'

'Newham, I thought.'

'Same difference. You couldn't make it up. Mel says she's decided to do her bit for Blighty and have as many as she can. She met this Italian family at Hurlingham, a tall, handsome well-dressed chap with a wife with an hour-glass figure to die for, who she assumed had no offspring. Turns out they had thirteen. Thirteen! The whole lot stuck together in a flat in Baron's Court, you can watch them on the internet.'

'They must have had a great lockdown! Is that what gave Mel the idea?'

'Ivan's always wanted a big family. He never said so straight out but I could tell. I'd have gone on too, but Carol thought three was quite enough.'

'I don't blame her. Do you know what women go through in childbirth?'

'Not bloody likely. I kept well away from all that. Carol didn't want me anywhere near her. You should have taken that half on nine when I offered it,' Bill added, suddenly changing the subject. 'You had fuck all to lose.'

Pete shook his head. 'You know what Joe Carr said? A gimme's a gentleman's agreement between two born losers.'

'Exactly.'

'And we're not losers.'

'Anything but.'

Bill struggled to his feet, but when Pete offered him a hand, he waved it aside.

'Never thought I'd live long enough...' Bill started, walking away.

'Long enough for what?' Bill shook his head. 'Never thought I'd see the day...' His sentence tailed off into the blackness.

As they pushed their heavy trolleys back towards the clubhouse, Pete heard a familiar, weary sigh.

'Pimms in paper cups. I ask you! What the fuck is the world coming to?'

What indeed!